Nephilim

Nephilim

The Seventh Angel

BERNETTE FORDE

Library of Congress Control Number: 2014912833
ISBN: Hardcover   978-1-4990-8816-8
               Softcover   978-1-4990-8817-5
               eBook   978-1-4990-8818-2

This book was printed in the United States of America.

Rev. date: 08/04/2014

To order additional copies of this book, contact:
Xlibris LLC
0-800-056-3182
www.xlibrispublishing.co.uk
Orders@xlibrispublishing.co.uk
635577

Dedicated to

Ivy Albertha Tucker, who has left her fingerprint
of grace in my heart and her wings upon my
soul. You will never, ever be forgotten.

Also

To my wonderful husband, Michael Forde. Thank you
very much for your time and patience during this process.

Acknowledgements

I'D LIKE TO acknowledge the Forde family for the wealth of information they supplied me for this book in reference to Ireland.

Also, I like to acknowledge:

Danette Robinson, D. J. Robinson, O. J. Robinson, Kalai Robinson, Nathan Robinson, Kalique Robinson, and Sarah Robinson

Michael Forde, Martin Forde, Sinead Forde, Sarah Forde and Karen Forde

James Barrett

Margaret Cumberbatch

Juanita Nisbett

Marion Dillworth

Lynette Tucker

Alphonso Tucker

My Facebook family and Kaneva family

Ali Riviera, Randy Smith, Jean Reeves and the whole Xlibris Family

May God Bless You All

Prologue

IT WAS GOING to be one of those long nights, with Sharon not knowing if she wanted to be a member of this society or not. She had often contemplated killing herself. Just so, the pain would go away. She hated these feelings of despair. However, unlike usual, this seemed to be more pressing than before.

Tonight was different from the other nights when she felt desperate and alone. There was so much more on her mind tonight. Her head needed to be clear. She now regretted so many decisions that she had made earlier, so much that had affected people in a negative way. This was the first time she had felt shame like this, shame and despair. Sharon did not think she was depressed. Depressed people would feel sadness, anxiety, emptiness, hopelessness, worry, or helplessness. She did not feel those things.

Maybe she would overcome these feelings just like before. What did she do before to come out of her despair? How did she feel after? Was she happy? Contemplating suicide was one of God's biggest sins. Not that she was ever a religious person, but she was aware she was not going to heaven if she followed through with her plans. However, there was this inner voice, prompting her, coaching her, forcing her a little maybe. She could feel it. It was like an angelic voice telling her to hurry and take the pills. She picked the pills up off the table and looked at the label.

It had her name on it still, but the contents inside was a mixture of all pills Sharon could find, assorted caplets and tablets with different colours and shapes. Some had been expired for well over a year, but she did not care, by any means necessary. So long as the end, result was what she hoped.

Sharon rose up from the couch she had been sulking. She slowly strolled over to the bar she had installed into the wall about a year ago. It was her dream bar. She had access to the bar from two rooms. The bar faced the entrance hall as you walked into her house. The other side of the bar faced the living room. She had talked to dozens of carpenters until she found the right one who could understand her vision for the perfect bar. No one in the world had a bar like Sharon's bar, glass and silver on the outside. Silver bar stools hugged the bar both inside the entrance as well as in the living room. There were tall glass pillars on each end, holding a crystal ball. A large chandelier filled with fine liquors at the base of each light fell over the bar. A pillar in the middle of the bar was home to a picture of her father on the entrance side and her mother on the living room side.

She went behind the bar and ran her fingers under the counter until she found the button she was looking for. When she pushed the button, a secret stash of alcohol slid out from the wall. These were her special wines. They would go well with the pill concoction she had in her hand. No one got these wines in the hidden stash.

Sharon grabbed the bottle of A. R. Lenoble 1996 Blanc de Blanc. That would be the last champagne she would want before she died. A. R Lenoble is a French sparkling white wine. A. R stands for Armand Raphael, who founded the company that made this fine champagne in 1920. Lenoble was the chosen name because he believed that champagne was the most noble of wines. Sharon agreed with this. The harmony of all the elements and intensity of flavour made this champagne a standout. She poured a generous amount into her glass and took a big swig of the intensifying liquid. This would calm her nerves and make the event a lot easier. Sharon loved the way it went down her throat, smooth.

She walked about the apartment while drinking champagne. She stared at her parents' pictures on the pillar, wondering what they would think if they knew of her turmoil. Surely, her mom would try to talk to her out of anything stupid; however, her dad would have shrugged his shoulders and say, 'Oh well.' As long as whatever his kids did did not affect him directly in a negative way, he would not have cared.

The time was at hand. She could feel the effects of the champagne. It was making her more miserable when she thought back into her life. Tears were starting to flow, thus making it easier to fulfil her intentions. All the pain and rejections and humiliations and every miserable thing that ever happened to her had surfaced. She spilt the bottle of pills out on to the bar and looked down at them. She picked up three or four tablets and placed them in her hand. She was about to pop the pills into her mouth when, through her tears, she saw to the right a sliver of rainbow light.

She turned to look at what had gotten her attention. On the floor was a swirl of light spinning. *WHAT is that?* She gasped as the light got bigger and bigger as it swirled around.

'What in tar nation is that?' she asked aloud. She stared at the light as it got taller and began to take form of a man. He was floating there surrounded by a light green mist.

She became frozen with fear. Maybe she was drunk. Was she seeing things? She could not stop staring at it. 'Oh my God! Heaven, help me,' she said aloud not realising it. She dropped the pills back on the table, and they spilt all over the floor. She slowly stood up. Should she run? She looked around the room for a place to run. No, she would not run. She had to face her demons. She walked towards the light and then heard a voice as loud as ever say. 'DO NOT

MOVE,' the voice boomed. She stopped in her tracks and stared about the room. *What is going on? Did this entity just spoke to me?*

She turned to look towards the entrance, and there was not a soul there. She turned and looked back into the living room and watched this thing staring back at her. Where did he come from? He was dressed in a robe of many pastille colours. His skin colour was pinkish. He was neither a white man nor a black man. He definitely was Indian or Mallotta. His long hair was brushed back into a ponytail. He had eyes that bore through her soul. She felt a burning sensation in her chest. She stared at him as her head began to swim.

Sweat beads poured off her face. Did she take the pills and this was the effect of dying or maybe she was just drunk? Her knees began to buckle beneath her. She was feeling weak, confused, and disorientated. There was black spots in her vision and ringing in her ears. *What is happening to me?* She could feel the hair standing up on the back of her neck. When her eyes closed, the room began to swim all around her, and she did not see the man standing over her, staring down at her. She collapsed down on the ground as she fainted, and her conscious mind fell into oblivion . . .

Chapter One

Danny McGregor

DANNY WAS BORN and raised in a small town in Indiana, but was of Scottish origin. He was a tall, muscular-built man, but slightly overweight. Slightly balding with curly hair on the sides gave him a distinctive look. He certainly had been able to turn a woman's head in his younger days. His habit consisted of cracking his fingers, which annoyed his wife and others around him. He had been happily married now for almost ten years, with four wonderful children. He worked as a taxi driver to support his growing family.

With the decline in the economy, the light at the end of the tunnel had been turned off for Danny. He had massive debts and rising. His wife didn't know about the debts, and he wanted to pay them off before she ever found out. Besides, he couldn't find it in himself to tell her. A man accepts to take guardianship of his family once he has married and created new lives. It was all about pride for him.

When the opportunity came across for him to make extra money on the side, he leapt at the chance. While sitting in his cab waiting for a fare to come along, his eyes caught an advertisement in the paper looking for people to be guinea pigs for this new experimental drug. It was a new company providing this opportunity, and it was secure as the guinea pig was protected and there was an antidote for the drug if things grew out of control.

The salary was 3,000 dollars for the first initial visit and one and a half grand for any subsequent visits thereafter. Danny circled the ad and promised himself that he would make contact. He had a few jobs that night and then went home thinking about the experiment. He had made up his mind. He would go first thing in the morning.

He walked into the office the next morning for more information on this opportunity. There, he was joined by a group of people also looking for information. There was a man dressed in a white coat talking to them. Danny slipped in and sat at the back of the group. The scene was all very professional looking and very clean. He got there just in time to hear what this doctor had to say.

'It's a mind-altering drug. The purpose of this drug is to change people's thoughts after using LSD or any other illegal drugs. Lots of addicts return to drugs after being successfully clean. But what makes them return for that high? It's got to be in the mind. Our company's aim is to help them not want to return. Not want to feel what drugs do to them. Are there any questions?'

'When can we start?' asked Danny?

'Today if you like. All you have to do is fill out these forms and give us permission to inject you. A nurse will be standing beside you with the antidote the whole time. You will also be monitored every step of the way. The drug stays in your system for approximately eight hours. We give you plenty of water to drink after four hours. This will give your body a chance to clean out all traces before you leave here today. Upon the seventh hour, a team of our specialist interviews you to find out what and if any moods changed. All you have to do is be honest and let them know if you felt or experienced any or the following mixed or sad emotions or if you became frightened. Let them know how you're feeling and what you experienced during the first four hours. If for any reason, you're uncomfortable before time is up, just say so, and the antidote will be administered immediately.'

'So after eight hours, I can be out of here and back to work? I drive cab and need to work this evening,' he informed him.

'Yes, you can return to your normal life. There is no dizziness or side effects what so ever. You will get the results of the study upon your next visit. And if you don't have a second visit, we will mail the results to you. We plan to release the study of this drug to the public in about three or four months, and we may call upon you to stand beside us in any news press.'

Danny was not interested in all that. He just wanted the money, and the sooner the better to get this done and over with. He had no interest in finding out more about the company. They looked legitimate enough with their clean professional office. If they had an antidote to jump in and save him from malfunctioning, he was happy. *Just give me the dang drug already, and let's get it over with,* he thought to himself.

'And when are we paid for being a guinea pig?' someone else asked. That was going to be Danny's next question. He must have been reading his mind.

'You're paid at the end of the full eight hours, after we are satisfied you're OK and there are no problems. We have done about six experiments so far, and not one person has returned to complain about anything. I would say it's been a success. So, if anyone of you wants to start this morning, please follow me. All others can leave their name and address, and we will mail you more details,' he informed them.

Danny rose up to follow the doctor into another room. Another man and a woman pursued behind him. Once inside the room, he saw a nurse sitting behind a desk. She passed them each a clipboard with forms attached and asked them to fill out all the forms.

'Make sure every question is answered and all your information is properly completed. Once this is complete, bring them to me, and I will take you to the study room. You may leave on your clothes, but make sure you have removed all jewellery.'

'Why?' asked the woman subject.

'It's just a precaution. Last week, a patient was so bored with the process. He fell asleep and struck his arm on the table, breaking the glass on his watch. We will not be responsible, so we put jewellery in safe keeping. I will be back to retrieve you in a few minutes. Please sit here to fill out your forms.'

Danny noticed that the questions appeared to be regular questions before any normal medical procedures. It looked like a pre-assessment questionnaire you might find in a clinic:

general health and fitness questions such as any serious illnesses you might have, chest pains, shortness of breath, any medicines you were taking, any allergies, drink alcohol, smoke, and recreational drugs. It all seemed pretty standard. He wasted no time in filling out all the necessary forms. He was as healthy as a horse.

Danny was anxious and wanted the procedure done and over with. He needed to pay some bills before the creditors came visiting his house. He was determined to be the first one in and the first one out with cash in his hands. He was pacing the room cracking his fingers, waiting for the nurse to come back. It was annoying the other two, but he didn't care. Looking at his watch wishing for time to race along, he started to huff and puff and showed his annoyance at their lack of rush. Just then, the nurse returned and seemed surprised that Danny had finished his questionnaire.

She picked up his papers and said, 'Mr McGregor, please follow me this way.'

And off they went. He was about to get some kind of substance shot into his veins, but at the end of the day, he would be a whole lot richer.

He was excited and silently calculating money in his head. What bill would he pay first? Which ones were more important? He couldn't help but see the proud smiles on his family's face when they saw that all the bills were being paid, on time. It was a wonderful thing when a man could provide for his family.

'Mr McGregor, please pay attention, sir. Have a seat on the end of the bed and roll up your sleeve,' the nurse ordered him.

Jarring himself back to reality, he hopped upon the bed and did as he was told. He didn't really want to have a conversation with this woman, but he couldn't help but ask her, 'Exactly how long have you been injecting people?'

'I am very qualified, sir, if that's what you're asking. I have been a nurse for twenty years. However, I have been working for this company for about six months. Rest assured, you are in good hands, sir.'

Was she being sarcastic? he wondered to himself. He didn't like sarcastic people. *Please God, let this day be over quickly.*

'OK, sir, here we go. You will feel a little prick. It will be all but two seconds. It's just the IV preparation for when the doctor administers the drug. He will be in shortly. A tray will arrive for you in about thirty minutes. There will be a mask, in case you want to relax. Magazines, food, and water will also be provided. Bathroom is to your left if you need to go anytime. You will have to wheel the IV with you. I will be sitting right over there if you need anything that's not provided on the tray.'

She hooked up the IV to his left arm and then propped up his pillows. She quickly left him and went off to prepare the other patients.

Danny looked about the room. It looked exactly like one of the emergency rooms you would find at any hospital. Everything was so clean and white. He relaxed and sat back on the pillows. Closing his eyes, his mind returned to dividing out the money between his creditors.

There was a sound that made him open his eyes. He turned his head to see about four people enter the room including the doctor and the nurse. They surrounded his bed and informed him that they were about to give him intravenous therapy.

'We will infuse the drug with glucose directly into your veins. This is done by what is called a drip. We are using a drip chamber, which prevents air from entering the blood stream. This way we can control the flow rate. The intravenous route is the fastest way to deliver this test drug. If at any time you're uncomfortable, let us know. The nurse will be here with you at all times, and we will be behind that window over there. Any questions, Mr McGregor?' asked the doctor.

'No, no questions. I am as ready as I'll ever get. You can begin to drug me up. Don't worry, if I don't like it, you will know.' Danny just wanted to hurry and get it over with. There was no need for chit-chat.

The doctor looked at everyone in the room and said, 'All right then, Paul, you may begin.'

Danny stared up into the ceiling, waiting for the worst to happen. He was getting frightened, but it was too late to back out now. He swore he could hear the ticking of someone's watch. It wasn't his watch, for they took his.

Thirty minutes later, he was still lying in wait. The door opened, and another man walked in with a tray. He hovered over his bed and called his name. 'Danny, here you go. Here is some food and goodies for you.' Danny couldn't believe it. It had been thirty minutes already. He sat completely straight up and concentrated on his body. He felt absolutely nothing, physically and mentally. Actually, he felt normal.

With a big grin, he said to the doctor, 'Hey, Doc! I don't feel a thing.'

'That's good, Mr McGregor. We are going to go now and monitor you from behind that window.' Patting Danny on the leg, they left the room. The nurse sat on the chair in the room and picked up a book.

Danny looked on the tray and decided to put the mask over his eyes and lay down to rest and continued to mentally work out his payment plans.

He was awoken exactly seven hours later. The nurse was shaking him gently. 'Mr McGregor, time to get up.'

Blinking his eyes, Danny pulled himself up into a sitting position. Again, the same people were in the room, surrounding his bed.

'How are you feeling, Danny?' asked the doctor.

'I feel the same way I do after a good night's sleep,' said Danny.

After a series of questions asked by the doctors, Danny was given plenty of water to drink and told he was ready to go home. He used the bathroom because it felt like his bladder was going to burst.

Another hour later, Danny was standing on the kerb outside the clinic with 3,000 dollars in his pocket. He was elated and thankful and relieved all at the same time.

As he walked to his taxi, he didn't notice the men at the window watching him. They all agreed that Danny would be back for more testing. They had given him no drugs at all. It was all glucose he had, no mind-altering drugs at all. The only thing the team of doctors injected him with was sugar.

They liked him for their real ultimate test. Their plan was to gain his trust, and indeed, Danny trusted them.

As long as Danny had the money in his pocket and he felt absolutely no side effects of the 'drug' he was given, he'd trust them. When they released this miracle drug to the public and the press asked him his view, he could honestly say it was a safe drug. Any ex-drug addict, given this miracle drug, would not return to street drugs.

Danny had not told his family yet about donating his body for drug testing. He had decided to pay all the small bills first and get them off his back. He was now down to just one big bill. Over a thousand dollars he owed on his credit card. One last visit for drug testing would take care of that bill in its entirety, and he would be debt free. This would be his third and last visit. He knew the procedure now, and he felt like an expert.

He planned on taking his wife out to dinner tonight to celebrate. There he would tell her everything. From all the debts right up to how he was able to get them out of debt. He envisioned the proud look on her face. She would be so thrilled about him.

Danny pulled up in front of the clinic. He was whistling as he parked the car. He was in a good mood and only expected it to get better. As he locked his car door, he was thinking about getting himself some new clothes. He thought maybe a pair of jeans and a new cardigan. He deserved to treat himself to new clothes after all the stress he went through. He even had enough to spare after the bills to treat his wife with a pair of earrings.

Danny was so deep in thought; he hadn't noticed the men at the window watching him. He had no inkling these men where planning his last visit with them as well.

Danny went through the usual routine of administering the drug. He continued to whistle as he relaxed in preparation for the next eight hours. He laid his head back and put the mask over his eyes and began to visualise his dinner tonight with his wife. He must have fallen asleep because the next thing he remembered was waking up and realising he had important business to take care of.

Only two hours had passed by, but Danny did not know this. He just felt a bit strange but very much aware of his thoughts and actions. He slowly got off the bed and went towards the door. He needed to leave. He didn't know why but just that he had somewhere to go.

Looking down in his hand, he saw his money. He counted it, and it was the 1,000 dollars for his pay today. However, that didn't seem at all important any more. He walked right out the clinic and into his cab. There, he sat for a moment and thought about what he had to do. He searched into his pockets and noticed he had a plane ticket along with his passport. Looking at the ticket, he knew where and why he had to travel today. He was going to Bermuda.

Danny drove himself to the airport and was on the next plane. He had never left the United States in his life, but somehow, he felt like an everyday traveller. He was focused and determined.

Chapter Two

Christine and Martin Lynch, Bermuda

CHRISTINE LYNCH WAS a native-born Bermudian, and her husband, Martin, was born in Ireland. They were a very happy couple and only had one or two arguments in their marriage. Talk about when opposites attract, it was them. She was brown skin, tall, and beautiful. He was the same height as his wife, but his skin was almost lily-white. Being born in Ireland, exposure to the cold, rainy weather made his skin white. With her Indian/Bermudian heritage, Christine had a light brown colour skin.

They never had any racial prejudice opinions thrown at them due to their different races or cultural backgrounds.

They decided to settle in Bermuda because it was her home. Christine wasn't into long distance travelling. She hated it with a passion. She was afraid of flying and heights. So the less travelling was better for her. Bermuda's closest point to the United States was less than two hours away from most US airports. They owned a holiday home in Miami, but they both loved Bermuda. Not to mention the beauty of the island, Bermuda is filled with palm trees and pink sandy beaches and the bluest water in the world.

Only twenty-five square miles, the island is surrounded by coral reefs that harbour colourful tropical fish and ensnared scores of shipwrecks.

Bermuda is known for its unexpected treasures and shipwrecks and historic sites. This has allowed for memorable diving and snorkelling. Bermuda also houses one of Britain's oldest preserved colonial towns in the world. Most homes and businesses consist of pastel-painted buildings, making a beautiful postcard picture.

Its people are very friendly and warm. *Condé Nast Traveler's* readers had voted Bermuda as the 'Best Island in the Caribbean'. Mark Twain once said, 'You go to heaven if you want—I'd rather stay right here in Bermuda.' Michael Douglas and Catherine Zeta-Jones once called Bermuda home and was a neighbour of the Lynches.

Christine and Martin loved their home and wanted to raise their daughters in Bermuda. They had two girls, Sharon and Karen. They were a year apart in age, clocking in at seven and six years old. Both girls attended primary school, and Martin and Christine took their parenting responsibilities to a whole new level and followed their every move. They watched them like a hawk.

They dropped them off at school as well as picked them up. Not once did they ever allow someone else to do that chore. Not once would you have ever seen the girls alone. They would give their own lives to protect both girls. It was their destiny to have the girls reach adulthood without any traumatic incidents.

Christine had not been sleeping very well lately. She had always been sick from one ailment or another, so sleeping had been difficult for her. This was going to prove to save them all one day. Years later, Sharon was told what actually took place that night. How Christine's night sweats had saved all their lives. It was a miracle they were still here today.

Christine could not sleep. That was nothing unusual. Tonight, like most nights, she tossed and turned. Finally, she decided to go use the bathroom and then wipe off some of the night sweat. She had been having hot flashes causing her not to sleep properly. Often the sheets would be soaking wet from her sweating.

Christine went into the bathroom. She washed her face and then took the towel to wipe her face and then her neck. As she looked at herself in the mirror, she felt she was getting old. Seems to her that every day, she would wake and there was another mole or wrinkle on her face. Christine was getting older. She sighed as she put away the towel.

Christine walked into the kitchen and looked at the clock on the wall. It was just after 4 a.m. Darn, another sleepless night. When was this ever going to end? She decided to take a couple of Tylenol time releases and go back to bed. She looked in on Sharon and Karen. They were both fast asleep. Christine crept back into bed, not wanting to wake her husband. She lay there begging sleep to come to her. As she waited, a sound reached her ears. What was that? She sat up in the bed. Listening, she heard the noise again. It was coming from the front door.

She got back out of bed and walked by the bedroom door, where she stood and listened. There it was again! Sounds like someone was fiddling at the door lock. Christine ran and jumped on the bed to wake her husband. Shaking Martin with a force she didn't even know she had, she shouted to him, 'Wake up. Someone is trying to break into the house.'

Martin was a light sleeper and woke immediately. 'Are you sure?' he asked her. But then he looked at the expression on her face. 'OK, I will go check it out,' he said.

'No!' Christine shouted. 'We will go check it out together.' They both went to the front door. Martin whispered to Christine that he would turn on the outside light and at the same time she would have to raise the nightshade. She whispered back OK.

Martin turned on the outside light and Christine raised the shade. And yes! There was a man there. He was on his knees with some kind of tools working on the locks. He was stunned when he saw Martin and Christine looking down on him. He didn't move though, and Martin was sure he'd run away once the lights turned on.

The man was Danny McGregor. He raised his head and looked at the Lynches for a moment and then returned to look at what he was doing as if he hadn't even seen them. Danny had a determined look on his face so Martin dropped the shade back down and turned to his wife.

'Quickly, call 911 and wake the kids. Hurry!' he whispered.

Christine ran to the kitchen, yanked the cordless from the base, and continued to run to the kids' room. She woke both girls and told them there was an intruder attempting to break into the house and to dress quickly. The girls didn't waste any time. They quickly dressed as their mother called the police. She told the operator that a man was breaking in and that her husband was at the front door monitoring his progress. She also told them that the man knew they were aware of his presence and did not stop. The 911 operator asked, 'Is there another way out of the house?'

'Yes,' Christine said. 'Should we go out through the back door?'

'You should and hide somewhere. The police are halfway there. Tell your husband to move away from the door and go

with you. Rest the phone down somewhere, but do not hang
up. The police should be there in less than five minutes.
OK . . . Now go!'

Christine whispered OK into the phone and rested it
on the coffee table and looked at her husband. She noticed
he looked very concerned and looked at the top lock on the
door. It was turned, and he flicked it with his finger, and it
spun around. The man had broken it and was working on
the doorknob lock. Christine signalled to her husband to
follow her. She had two pairs of jeans in her hand.

They quickly moved towards the girls' room and took
their kids by the hands and slipped quietly out the back door.
Martin gently closed the door behind them.

They could hear sirens in the distance. Relieved to hear
them, they looked around. To the right of their backyard was
a wall that separated them from the neighbours. They helped
the girls crawl over the wall and jump the wall themselves.

The neighbour's sensor light clicked on so they ran
around the house and on to the main road. They could see
the flashing lights and ran towards it. The police officer saw
them waving and screeched to a halt.

'Are you the family that's in trouble?'

'Yes, we are, and the man is still at our front door trying to get in,' screamed Martin.

'OK. See the bushes over there, go behind them, and don't move until you're called to come out,' he shouted at them.

Martin gathered his family and headed towards the bushes. There, Christine and Martin put their jeans on over their pyjamas and tucked in the PJ top into their jeans. Karen's curiosity got the better of her and asked, 'Dad, what's going on?'

'We are not sure, honey,' he replied. 'We just have to stay here until the police comes to tell us it's safe to go back home.'

Martin got on his knees and hugged Karen into his arms while Christine cuddled Sharon, hoping to comfort the girls. Martin stuck his head into the bush, trying to see the police's progress in capturing the burglar.

As the police drove up to the Lynches' home, they saw the intruder break the lock and enter the house. He stood in the doorway and turned to see the police officers. He looked like a man on drugs or something so they decided to call for back-up.

One officer stepped out of the car while the other called it in. 'This is Officer Smith. Officer Robinson and I need back-up to the Lynch's address. Something weird is going on here. The intruder is not running away, knowing full well we are here.' Officer Smith yelled into the radio.

Officer Robinson called on his bullhorn for the intruder to come out of the house, but he ignored that, and the police saw all the lights turned on in the house. What was he looking for? They could see him clearly walking around in the house from room to room as if looking for something. The first officer leant in the window and said to Officer Smith calling it in.

'Better tell them to hurry. I don't like this!'

'Dispatch, we have a 10-66. Can you hurry with that back-up? We are feeling crept out by this guy.'

'Back-up is one minute behind you. They see your lights flashing.'

Just then, about three police cars drove up alongside the first attending officers. A total of six officers were on the scene. They were all filled in on the events and watched as Danny walked about the house. Then he stood at the door looking at the officers. One of the officers shouted at him to turn around and lie on the ground. Of course, that would be too easy because the man walked towards them without a care in the world. He was told again to halt and drop to the ground.

'We don't want to have to use force on you. Just do as you're told and lie on the ground.'

Danny stopped and stared at them.
'I just want the family that was here. If you tell me where they are, I won't use force on you!' shouted this guy.

'What could you possibly want with that family?' asked one of the officers.

'I have to kill the little girls who live in that house,' he calmly told them.

This revelation put all officers on alert. Officer Robinson jumped back into his car to retrieve his rifle, while Officer Smith called for more officers.

'Dispatch 11-99 to the Lynch's address, pronto!' he shouted into his radio.
Danny walked closer to the officers and asked again, 'Where is the family?' He shouted. One of the officers walked up to Danny because he saw no weapon in his hands. He

told him to don't be a fool and just surrender to them. The man snatched him by the neck and squeezed.

'I WANT THAT FAMILY!' he shouted at them.

'Err, dispatch change that to a code 30! We have an officer in trouble. Send as much as possible!'

Officer Smith knew it was going to take more than six officers to bring him down. Another officer used his taser on Danny, but this did nothing to him. So three more tasers were used and still nothing. He sure was a strong guy.

'Dispatch, where are my officers I called for? This guy is not going down. He must be high on something.'

'We may have to use another method to bring him down, for the safety of the officers.'

'Copy that. Be advised, permission granted by the CO. Units are on the way,' chirped dispatch!

Once permission had been granted, officers were allowed to shoot, maybe a leg or arm, to bring down the suspect. Failing that, the heart or head had become the target.

With guns now drawn, Officer Robinson shouted at Danny, 'Last warning, drop to the ground, or you WILL be shot!'

Danny ignored him and continued to fight with the officers. He was being tased by them all at this point, but he wasn't going down. Officer Smith shouted to the other officers to back away. Then they all noticed that the first officer Danny had in his grip was slumped to the ground. Officer Smith looked at his comrade on the ground and then looked back at Danny.

He fired off a shot into his left leg and then a second shot into his right arm. Danny didn't even flinch. His attention had been drawn to a bush down the road across the street. People had come out of their homes to watch by this time, but Danny was not bothered by anyone along the road. It was the bush that had his focus.

Officer Smith's eyes followed his gaze, and he realised that was where the family had been told to get out of sight. There was movement in the bush, and he knew he had to take down Danny before he got to those girls. Danny walked towards his target and then broke out into a run.

Officer Smith shouted, 'Fire at will! Bring him down before he reaches that bush!' All officers started shooting at Danny as he ran down the road.

He finally dropped right in front of the bush. Officer Smith reached him and leant down to turn him over. Danny was still alive and stared at Officer Smith. He was trying to say something, so Officer Smith bent over to hear him clearer.

He heard him clearly say, 'One of those girls MUST die tonight. I don't know which one so both must die. I have failed my mission. You must do it. This is on your shoulders now.' With that said, his eyes closed, and he died.

The bush was rustling again, and out of nowhere came a cat. Officer Smith looked behind the bush, and the family was not there. He rushed back over to the first officer slumped over to find out he also had passed away. He had been strangled.

What had happened here? Where did the family go? Smith took a deep breath and walked to his car, dreading the report he would have to write up.

Martin had watched the scene from between the bush and realised this guy was determined to get them. Danny wasn't abiding by the officers' commands. He decided to move his family away from the scene before it got worst. He noticed people appearing all over the place, wondering what was going on.

He decided the best way to hide was in plain sight. He whispered to Christine to creep along the ground with the girls and to follow him. Martin stayed low and crept along the grass over to a long row of bushes. He looked behind him to see his ladies following him. *Good*, he thought.

When he reached the wall, he stood up and walked behind a neighbour's house. Once all were there, they casually walked out of the darkness and stood by the roadside with the other onlookers. As he watched, he couldn't believe his eyes. Who the hell was this guy and what did he want with his family?

Thank God, Christine had night sweats; otherwise, he was sure they'd all be dead. Martin looked up and down the road looking for the officer who had instructed him to protect his family. It looked like the officer had gone. Martin decided to return to the house. He could plainly see the man was dead and not about to hurt anyone.

As he walked up to the door, he saw the traditional yellow tape going across his door. He ripped it down and entered his house. After settling the girls back into bed, Martin and Christine sat on the couch to discuss their next move. There was a gentle knock at the door, and it was the police. They were not happy to see the Lynches in the house.

'Sir, you are not supposed to be here. Officer Smith has been looking for you.'

'We are not leaving our home. The girls are back into bed, so you can call Officer Smith and let him know we are here. We are not going anywhere tonight,' he informed them.

The officer called it in and told them the Lynch family was back in the home. The decision was made to let them remain and the place would be watched for the remainder of the night. Martin and Christene could not go back to sleep. They instead sat up and had their coffee, discussing what their next move should be. They knew this would not be the last attempt on their girls' lives.

Chapter Three

Sharon Lynch
Twenty Years Later

S HARON FELT THE heat along her face as the summer
sun streamed across her pillow. She opened her eyes to
a strangely quiet house. The place was serene and peaceful,
and therefore, the sole interruption was a ticking clock.
Rubbing her eyes, it took a minute to register where she was
and for her eyes to adjust to the room. She looked around
and realised she was in her bed. Sharon leant over to check
the time; it was just past 9 a.m. She had never slept this late
before. Whoa! What a nightmare that was she had last night.

Damn girl, you got to stop attempting to end your life! she
mentally scolded herself. She never succeeded in that mission
and always never remembered going to bed. The last she
remembered was sitting at her bar drinking champagne.
She must have drunk the whole bottle for the way her head

___ now. Her body felt sort of, like a truck ran over her. She looked down at her body, and she was full of bruises.

What the hell? she thought to herself. She got out of bed and went into the bathroom. She looked in the mirror and saw bruises all over her body, even on her face. She looked seriously beat up, but there was no blood. Her skin had not been broken. She threw on the clothes she found on the floor. Even though she woke in her own bed, it was not crumpled, and she did not move much through the night. It seemed as if somebody had put her there.

When she opened her bedroom door, she heard what sounded like toast popping out the toaster. Someone was in her kitchen. She strolled towards the kitchen and then saw this man standing at her stove. She stared at him and wondered who he was. Did she pick him up in a bar or something? She just did not remember. She watched him with a keen eye. He had on blue jeans and a T-shirt with writings on it; she had never seen before in her life. He turned around with the frying pan in one hand and a spatula in the other and noticed her standing in the doorway looking at him.

'Good morning,' he chirped. However, she ignored his greeting and continued to look at him. She felt almost as if she was spying, but she knew she was in her home and he was the stranger. She chose not to speak to him yet and just observe. She stared at him as she walked around the kitchen, eyes not leaving his. She reached the knife block on the counter, stopped, and looked at him. There was a territorial look in her face. He never looked away from her and never released the hold of the pan with eggs in them.

She had on her clothes from the night before and looked a bit ragged. Her mascara had run a bit down her face from the tears she shed before and had dried on her face. She had bruises on both cheeks and had no idea how they got there. Her hair was pointed upwards in the air, suggesting a hard night's sleeps, but her bed said otherwise. She looked evil even, but he did not budge. She waited for his explanation without asking who he was. He offered absolutely nothing.

'Look, we can stay here all day looking at each other if you wish. On the other hand, we can eat some toast and eggs. We really do not have much time, though. May I suggest you eat something'?

She looked at him and wondered who was this man. She wondered about the nerve of him, suggesting she should eat something. *How dare he! Who is he?* Better still, she did not want to know. He best just would leave, and whatever happened last night would best to forget.

'Well, what do you say?' he asked.

She looked at him and said, 'Get out!'

He then knew he was on a difficult mission. It made no sense fighting with her. He decided to do just as she asked him. He could keep an eye on her at a distance. He put the pan back on the stove and turned off the heat. He pulled out all the plugs he put in. He took a sip of his coffee, then turned and looked at her. Without another word, he picked up something off the counter and walked out gently, shutting the door behind him.

Sharon breathed a sigh of relief. She did not want to have to pull out any knives from the knife block. She pattered across the floor towards the foyer to make sure he left. When she was sure he left, she checked all the windows and made sure they were secure. She took a shower and changed clothes. She needed that shower and could use a couple of painkillers as well. Her head was still pounding. She went into the kitchen and saw the eggs still sitting on the stove.

Wow! She would have to stop drinking if she was bringing home strange men. She had enough on her plate than to have to worry about some disease or something. She found tablets in the kitchen drawer and washed down two with some water. Hmmm, those eggs sure looked good. She decided not to waste them. Sitting down on the stool next to the kitchen island, she started her breakfast. Her mind had drifted back to the events of last night. Why was it that every time she tried to kill herself, somehow it did not happen. She was not supposed to be in here and now. Having failed (again) was not an option.

However, she was feeling a bit better about things today. Having a man in her apartment cooking her eggs really was somewhat nice. Now that would have been a first in her life. Too bad, he was a pickup from somewhere. When she thought back, he was handsome! His hair was wavy, long, and tied back into a ponytail. His eyes looked of Asian descent, but his skin tone was olive. She could not believe she kicked out a very handsome guy without waiting to find out who he was. He looked familiar, but she could not remember where she had seen him before.

Then, like a lightning bolt, it hit her. She never went out last night. She did not meet him in a bar and bring him home in a stupor. She was in her apartment all night alone, drinking and thinking about killing herself. She was drinking champagne and was about to pop some pills when . . . when . . . when what? Her mind was a complete blank. Oh, wait a minute. Wait a minute. Just what happened here last night?

She ran about the apartment in frenzy. Her last memory was in the living room. She dashed across the entrance and over to the bar. The pills were not there. She looked about the room. On the coffee table, there sat nothing but an empty plant pot she had been meaning to fill. She went behind the bar and pushed the button that showed her hidden treasure of fine wines. The bottle of Lenoble was gone. She went into the kitchen but could not find the empty bottle of champagne. Where did it go? The pills and the champagne were nowhere in sight. Puzzled, she decided to go outdoors for some fresh air. Maybe then she would remember what had gone on last night.

It was a warm day so she decided to go for a walk. She put on her knee-high hip huggers and a waist-length T-shirt. Sneakers would be nice and comfortable for a brisk walk. She got a couple of paper towels and folded them flat to place inside her cap. Rolling her long hair around her finger, she pulled the cap over her head and pushed the ponytail through the opening at the back. She loved wearing her cap that way when out walking. With the towel inside, it helped to absorb any dripping of perspiration. The park across the street would be perfect for her walk. It had a footpath around the whole park she could take and be back well within the hour. As she left, she saw two of her neighbours outside, chatting. They waved to her, and she waved back. There were only five houses in the neighbourhood. Hers was the fourth one, so she had to walk towards and past the two ladies.

As she got closer to them, they stopped chatting and looked at her. Their eyes followed her, and she wondered why they were looking at her. Then she remembered the bruises.

'Are you all right, Sharon?' one of them shouted.

'Yes, I fell,' Sharon lied.

Instantly, she got the feeling that they did not believe her. Did they know something Sharon did not? If only she could remember. However, she knew she would have to really find out what exactly happened to her. Otherwise, people would be asking all sorts of questions she could not answer. She jogged past them towards the park to get away quickly.

Once in the park, she stopped and looked around. The park had a few people milling about. It looked like a teacher with her class. Two lovers sat on a bench. A mom, on her blanket, was watching as two little kids played. There were walkers, joggers, and runners coming in and out of the footpath.

There was a man leaning against a tree reading the newspaper. Another man walked with his dog. The footpath had a scenic pedestrian route all the way around the park. All other sorts of traffic were prohibited. It had a nature trail with ponds and shrubs that ran along the edge of the path. There were tall trees so high that you could barely see the sky.

Sharon decided to go on the pedestrian footpath. It would be a great scenic route to take, and she could think about her day's events. She ran towards her destination and took her place on to the footpath behind a man and woman walking holding hands.

As she walked by, she got a clearer view of the man walking the dog. It looked like a guy named Carlton she used to work with a long time ago. They worked for a small hardware store as buyers, and their desks were close by each other. Wow, she thought. She had not seen him a long time. She walked along the path admiring the flowers and fish swimming about the pond.

Then she heard her name was called by someone. She looked in the direction and saw that indeed it was Carlton. He was calling her. He motioned her to come over towards him. She assumed he was waving at her so she waved to him and kept walking.

Half way through the park, she saw him again with his dog. This time the dog was not on his leash. Sharon did not like dogs and decided to sit down to see what the dog was going to do. It was a Cocker Spaniel. It walked right up to her and started to sniff at her feet. She felt like kicking it away, but she saw Carlton coming.

As he reached her, he pulled his dog away, apologising, 'Sorry about that, Sharon.' He put the leash back on. Patting his dog, he said, 'Sam would not hurt a fly.'

'Hello, Carlton. I do not like or trust dogs. However, I can see Sam is adorable! May I pat him?'

'Sure. Go right ahead. He will love it.'

Sharon reached out and scratched behind Sam's ears. The dog responded by licking her arms.

'So, Sharon, do you live around here?' he asked.

'Yea, not far from here, just around the corner really,' she told him.

'I live nearby too and come to the park everyday to walk Sam.'

She waited for him to ask about her bruises, but he did not. Instead, he asked if she would have coffee with him. She was surprised that he did not ask about her bruises. They were clearly visible.

'Sorry, Carlton, I cannot. I am busy today. I have to get back now. Nice seeing you, though, and thanks for asking.'

She stood up to walk away, but Carlton put his hand on her arm and stopped her.

'Really, you should have coffee with me,' he said. Sharon turned and looked at him.

'Really now, Carlton. I have not seen you in like how long, maybe five years if not more. You see me unexpectedly, and I must have coffee with you. I am flattered, but no thanks. Have a great day!'

She waved as she turned on her heels and skipped into a jog. *What is wrong with that guy?* she thought. He acted as if he did not even notice her bruises. The first things most people ask were 'what happened to you' or made some kind of mention about the bruises. Sharon decided to run faster and get back to the house. Maybe this was a bad idea after all.

As she ran along, she saw the man with the newspaper looking at her. Why was he looking at her so intently? She watched him fold his paper and started towards her. She could see the sweat pouring off him. She decided to turn to the north a little bit so she would not have to cross his path, but he saw this and moved to the north a bit too. *Oh, shit,* she thought, *something is just not right about this.* She decided to cut across a grassy knoll she saw.

Sharon ran right by the woman on the blanket with her kids. She looked behind her and noticed both Carlton and the man with the newspaper running behind her. *Are they chasing me? What is going on?* She put her long-distance running medals to use. Sharon broke out into a run and went as fast as she could.

She ran swiftly along the trail, dodging in and out of bushes trying to lose them. Then she noticed this large Osiria rose bush in full bloom. The roses on the bush had deep red insides and silver-white on the outside of each petal. It looked like an upright habit, with dark green leaves. Giving any other circumstance, Sharon would have stopped and inhaled the fragrance of hybrid tea the roses gave, but for now, she dove into the large bush. With the branches scratching her face and arms, she fell on to the ground and then scrambled on her knees to peep between the leaves to see where her pursuers were. She did not see them in any direction and was successful in losing them but decided to wait five minutes before coming out.

Sharon checked her watch and noticed eight minutes had passed. Looking around as she crept out of the shrubbery, heart beating wildly in her chest, Sharon stood up. She did not see anyone so she walked in the opposite direction she last saw them. With a sigh of relief, Sharon took off into a jog along the dirt footpath and took a sharp turn towards her house.

Her long ponytail was swaying left to right as she jogged along. Her shirt was drenched in sweat more from the fear she endured than from the actual running. Rocks were scraping against her white sketchers, leaving marks on the toe area. She sucked her teeth and lips. She was disappointed and frustrated that her sneaker got damaged, as they were her favourites.

Then she saw him, in front of her, another man searching and looking around. Was he looking for her? There was a platform designed for performance shows at the end of the trail. There were many trees behind the stage, and Sharon decided to run towards the stage to hide behind the trees. She saw her destination and picked up speed towards it when this man jumped out from behind a bush on to the trail. He had a gun in his hand. This took her by surprise and stunned her, making her jump back.

Adrenaline rushed up her spine. She felt her heart jump out of her body. *What to do? What to do?* she asked herself. Looking around, she decided to run to the right behind some trees. Running as fast as she could, she felt her muscles tense up in preparation for an endurance it seemed to know was coming. She was panting and begging God to let her get out of this alive. Pushing away any branches that hit her in the face, she jumped over obstacles in her way. Sharon was getting all scratched up as she ran, adding to the already bruises she had from whatever it was that attacked her the night before. She did not stop to look behind her to see how far away her new pursuer was. She felt like a tiger's prey, and he was the predator, stalking her, he seemed determined to catch her. She felt a breeze zoom past her head. He was shooting at her.

She turned to look and saw that he was in a position of aiming the gun at her. If this were in slow motion, she would have seen the bullet pass by her head. She decided her legs just had to save her life. She broke into a run knowing her life depended on her speed. Without looking behind her any more, she ran into a clearing and noticed an iron fence up ahead, and if she could just make it to the fence, she would climb it and jump to the other side.

The fence ran around the perimeter of the park, keeping the homeless and beggars out long after closing time. Sharon ran up to the fence and noticed it was a cast-iron fence. Using her gymnastic skills, she carefully put her foot into the groove between the two iron rods and pulled herself up. Careful to keep her hands over the top of the arrow-shaped points, she used all her strength to pull her body up and hoist her right leg over the fence. She slowly sat straddling the fence with her right leg on one side and her left leg dangling on the park side. She looked in the direction she just ran from to see his progress.

Moving slowly over the fence had clearly given him some time to get closer, but Sharon felt she still had more time before he could catch up. She turned her body slightly to the right, hoisted her left leg over the arrow point, covered both arrows with her hands, shoved her body over, and jumped to the ground.

She waited a few seconds to see if she had done any damage to her legs. Shaking them slightly, she noticed they were fine and darted into a run. After about a three-minute run, she slightly turned her head to see if he was following but did not see him near her. She slowed down into a jog and turned running backwards with her eyes searching for her pursuer. He was not following her. Squinting her eyes, she could see him still over the fence, but he was not climbing down.

She stopped, and straining her eyes further, she noticed this man was not just stuck but he was impaled on the fence. Then she heard his screams! She could hear the man's terrible screams echoing. He was hollering a harsh abrupt shrill cry like the sound of a wounded animal. People were entering the area as if they were there all along. Sharon felt safe enough to return.

As she got closer, she noticed he was a man in his fifties. Damn, someone should have told him he would not be able to make it over that fence. She sure wished she had her cellphone so she could take a few pictures, but she had left it on the table. She noticed a woman snapping pictures of the impaled man so Sharon started to walk over to her.

Then out of the corner of her eye, she saw Carlton and the other man with the newspaper walking towards the scene. She looked at the man impaled and saw that he was looking at her. Then their eyes met, and she could feel his pain and saw his frustration. For a fleeting moment, she felt sorry for him. Sharon backed up and decided to run away.

She ran out the park and down the street past her house. She saw the two ladies still there, chatting, but did not acknowledge them this time. Sharon did not see their eyes following her.

If these guys were chasing or following her, she did not want them to know where she lived. She ran towards the parking lot, knowing a police station was on the other side of the lot. She did not look back or stop until she passed the parking lot. She stopped just on the few steps leading into the police door.

Then she turned and looked back in the direction she came from. Yes, they were running through the parking lot towards her. Something made the guy with the paper to put his hand out in front of Carlton, and they both came to a stop. He had noticed the police station and decided not to follow her further. She saw his hesitation, and a smile came across her face. Raising her arm, she stuck her middle finger high up in the air at them both.

Unbeknown to her, someone else was watching out the police station, through second-storey window. Reid Sinclair worked for the Miami police for the past half dozen years now. He had been promoted to detective after only four years on the force and spent the final two years on the second floor in his office. He enjoyed his being on the higher floor as he loved to face out the window and observe the people bustling about.

It was one of these times when he was looking out, when he noticed a young woman who appeared to be jogging in the parking lot opposite the station. Upon a closer look, he realised she was moving towards the police building. He watched her intently. As she came nearer to the building, he noticed she had bruises on her face and arms. Glancing over the surroundings, he examined two men not too far behind her.

'What the hell?' he asked himself aloud.

He dropped down the pen he was holding and picked up his camera and snapped a few photos before rushing out the doorway.

Sharon shouted at them, 'What?'

However, of course they did not respond. She decided to go just inside the door a little and peep out through the small window in the police door. She watched them from there. They looked like they did not know what to do. They stood talking to each other. She watched them walk away towards a bench and sat down, but continued to stare towards the station. They were prepared to wait until she came out.

Well, Sharon was prepared to remain in her haven all night if she had to. She was not leaving until they were gone. They had to go soon. She wondered why they were chasing her. She had no enemies and had never crossed a person in her life.

Sharon jumped out of her skin when someone tapped her on her shoulders. 'Miss, are you OK?' She turned around to see this fair-skinned man looking at her. He had a nice tan and curly hair. She could not help but notice how handsome he was.

'I am fine. Thank you,' she replied, turning to look back out the window.

'You're all beat up and look to me like you're not fine and could use help. Are those men chasing you?'

'Are you a police officer?'

'Yes, I am. Detective Reid Sinclair. I was just about ready to finish work and go home. I looked out the window when I noticed you running in the parking lot. I was about to turn away, and then I noticed two guys running behind you and figured you needed help. I decided to take pictures.

'What's going on?' he asked her.

'Well, to tell you the truth, I don't have a clue what's going on. My name is Sharon. Sharon Lynch. I sure hope you can help me. This morning I woke up to a man in my house frying eggs. Still do not know who he was or what he was doing there. Then these two guys were chasing me in the park. One of them I used to work with five years ago and never saw since. Maybe if you did talk to them, I will know what's going on,' she said.

Reid looked towards the desk and motioned two officers to come over. They talked in low voices; then Reid said to her, 'Well, we will go out to chat with them guys.' Pointing to the officer behind the counter, he said, 'You go with that officer and file a complaint. Tell them everything that has happened in the last twenty-four hours.'

Sharon felt a dread in the pit of her stomach. She did not want to tell about the Lenoble and the tablets, the shame of it all. Well, she decided there and then not to reveal her intentions to end her life. All they needed to know was what she chose to inform them.

Peeping out the window, she watched as Reid walked towards the men sitting on the bench. Carlton tapped the other man to warn him the police was coming their way. They both stood up and walked in opposite directions. People had been walking all over the place blocking her view. They were blocking Reid's view too.

By the time he got near the bench, they were both gone. All they could do now was throw their hands up in the air and frown in disappointment. It was all right though because Reid had taken pictures from his window. He would get the lab to blow them up and run them through Avis. He wanted to help this beautiful woman in distress and felt the need to protect her. Who could have possibly bruised her like that?

An officer escorted her to a desk and told her to sit in the chair beside it. She was given a form and told to fill it in with all her information. *Oh, this is going to be easy,* she thought. Name: Sharon Marie Lynch. Age: Twenty-seven. Address: 842 Pearle Avenue, Miami Beach, Florida.

The Lynch family on her dad's side originated in Ireland, where that surname was most common. Her dad was Martin Joseph Lynch.

Her mom and dad married and settled in Bermuda, and this was where she grew up. However, Sharon moved to Florida and settled in Miami. She loved Miami. She felt at home there, and besides, her father's family immigrated there. Sharon wanted to visit home and see her parents, but she just did not have the time. Besides, if her mother found out about her depression, she would freak! She would want her to come home immediately and remain there.

Scanning the questions on the complaint form, she filled it out as much as she could. Then it asked her to say in her words what her complaint was. She had no clue what to write so she rested the forms on the table and sat on her hands. She looked around the room and noticed the police station as if for the first time. It was unusually busy for this time of day. The officers were all dress in their traditional navy police uniforms from Harrison Uniform & Police Supply at 3240 Seventh Street. Reid was not wearing a uniform so she thought he might be a detective. Just as she was thinking about him, he walked into the station and headed straight to her.

'Sorry, Miss Lynch, but those men disappeared right in front our eyes,' he said as he approached her.

'People were all over the place, and I could not see clearly. I do have their pictures though and can find out who they were. Did you fill out the complaint? The sooner you press charges, the quicker we can find and detain them.'

'I am having second thoughts about pressing charges. Maybe they just mistook me for someone else. I really do not want to cause any trouble for anyone. I will just head on home now,' she explained.

'Listen, Sharon, they will be back looking for you. I do not think they made a mistake. They followed you all the way to the police station. They were determined to catch you before you made it here. Guys do not do that as a mistake. You really have to let us find out why. If you do not know, then it is our job to find out. They may even be waiting for you to come home. Hell, they may even be in your house!'

'OK, OK, you're scaring me now. I will fill out the complaint. I just didn't have the words to describe what went down.'

'Well, I can help you with that. You tell us what happened, and I will write it out for you. All you will have to do is sign it.'

'I appreciate your help. My brain is so jumbled right now,' Sharon informed him.

About an hour later, with the necessary papers signed and filed, Reid could now actively work on this case. He just felt the need to help her. He decided to take her home himself instead of a regular unit.

'I do not live far from here. I am on Pearle Avenue. I can actually walk.'

'I will walk with you and make sure you get home safe,' he informed her.

He opened the door for her as they walked into the streets. He walked beside her, and they walked briskly along until he said, 'Tell me about the bruises. What happened to you?'

'Well, when I woke this morning, my body was all bruised like this. I do not remember a thing about last night. It's like I must have been in another world or something. I woke in my bed, but the bed was not crumpled. I found that very odd, so I thought maybe I had been placed there. Then I heard toast popping up from the toaster, so I went to the kitchen to have a look, and lo and behold, a man was there frying eggs. I have never seen him in my life, but he acted as if we were old friends or someone. I thought for a quick moment that I might have had too much to drink and done the "one-night stand thing", but that is not my character. I did not feel threatened by him, but I still was unsure as to whether to trust him or not.'

'Did he leave?' asked Reid.

'Oh yes. I gave him a stare that would have scared the whiskers of a panther. The weird thing is, he acted as if he did not want to leave. He even offered me a plate of breakfast. The nerve of him. He left though. I locked the house up tight after he left. Then I decided to go for a walk. I was not in the park for five minutes when Carlton came up to me and offered to buy me a cup of coffee. The cheek of him. Of course, I refused and walked away. Next thing I knew, he and that other guy were following me, so I ran. They chased me through the park, so I ran past my house and straight to the police station.'

'Why would a guy cook in your house if you didn't invite him to do so?' wondered Reid out loud.

'I don't know. I do not remember a thing.'

'Well, did you drink last night? Maybe you had too much.'

'I had a few glasses of wine, but I have drunk wine before and remembered every moment of it. Last night was different. Something really was not right last night. I admit

I have forgotten something, but I am sure it is not due to the wine. I was sitting on my couch one minute and then waking up the next in my bedroom the next morning. All I know is I never left my house yesterday at all.' She felt tears coming on.

Sharon and Reid were so engrossed in their conversation so they did not notice Carlton on the other side of the road. He was watching them intently. *Why did she have to bring that cop with her?* He would best call Brian to let him know that she was not alone.

'What, he is there?' Brian shouted into the phone. 'OK, come back here to the shop, and we will try to work out another plan.' Carlton shut his phone and put it into his pocket. He stared at the couple a few more minutes and then turned and walked away.

High above a tree across the street was another man watching as well. However, his object of attention was not Sharon but Carlton. He watched as Carlton walked away, and he too slipped away into the shadows.

Sharon and Reid reached her house, and he stopped and looked around for any signs of suspicious-looking characters lurking about. 'I think I'd feel better if I went inside and looked around if you don't mind,' said Reid. 'I really have a problem with the two guys chasing you earlier.'

'OK,' replied Sharon. 'I actually prefer if you did. I'd feel better too.' She gave him a bright smile.

Reid thought, *What a beautiful smile she has.* She had perfect teeth, grinning back at him. Her hair was pulled back into a tight bun. Her large brown eyes were staring at him. She made his heart lurch. He fought the urge to caress her bruises across her cheeks. Who would do such a thing to a beautiful woman? This was one mystery he was determined to solve. Even if she turned out to be some kind of nutcase, then he would assist her get the necessary help she might need. He felt that it was his responsibility to protect her. Moreover, indeed it was. After all, he was a cop.

He took the keys from Sharon and entered the house himself. As he entered the entrance foyer, he pulled out his gun and proceeded to walk about the house cautiously. She walked in behind him and stood there waiting for him to let her know it was safe to enter. He went into each room and stayed there for about thirty seconds, coming out shaking his head indicating no one was in there. An odd thought crossed her mind as she wondered if she had cleaned up after herself when she left to go for a walk. She could not remember and just hoped her room was clean.

He returned and said, 'All clear.' Sharon came all the way in and closed the front door behind her. She placed her keys on the small table by the door and proceeded to go into the kitchen. 'Would you like something cool to drink?' she asked.

'Sure. I could certainly use it after that walk and after what you told me. Please sit and tell me again. From start to finish.'

'Well, it all started last night. It was about 9 p.m. I think. I was sitting on my couch having a glass of wine. I remember having two glasses and about to have my third, and then there is a blank. Nothing at all comes to my mind. Then the next morning, I wake up in my bed. My clothes are on the floor. My body is all bruised.'

Sharon raised her sleeve and showed him the bruises on her arms. 'There are a few on my stomach and neck as well. Then I walk into the bathroom to check my entire body, and there are bruises all over. Very confused, I get dressed. Then I hear my toaster pop up and realise someone is in this kitchen. I quietly go by the kitchen door, and this man is standing by the stove frying eggs. He turns and sees me and acts as if we are friends. At first, I thought I might have gone out and had too much to drink and brought home a stranger. However, that is out of my character so I quickly squash that thought. I walk over to the knife block just in case I need to protect myself, and he says we do not have much time and I should eat breakfast. I am shocked and ask him to leave. He just looks at me and decides it best he leaves because he just picks up something off the counter and walks out. Then later, I decide to go for a walk in the park to freshen up my mind, and I run into Carlton who invites me for coffee. I decline and get the feeling he is not pleased, so I walk away. Nevertheless, he follows and then I notice that the other guy is following too. I run right past my house and to the police station. The rest is history as they say. That is it. That's my story.'

She sat down to the counter and indicated for Reid to do the same. She slid a glass of juice over to him.

'OK, so let's get this straight. You know the guy who chased you, right?' he asked.

'Yes, the smaller guy. I met him about five years ago in a hardware store. We both brought stock and supplies for the store. We were not close, but we were cordial to one another. If my memory serves me correct, I think his last name is Anderson.'

'So he is aware you know him. That is not good. He thinks you probably already told the police about him. I am going to run a check on him and also ask for a patrol car to remain outside your house this evening.'

Sharon was about to protest, but he raised his hand stopping her. The subject was closed. 'Don't you worry, Sharon. I will get to the bottom of this. Do you have any family here you can go to?'

'I have a younger sister. I see her from time to time. Maybe not as much as I should, but if I need to go somewhere, I can go there. She owns a store about five miles from here and lives above her store. I will be safe there. I will go there tomorrow if you have not picked up Carlton.'

'I like that idea. It's settled then. I am going to make some calls. You go about your day as if I am not even here.'

'OK, great.' Sharon thought this would be a good time for her to shower and feel safe. Therefore, she got up and went into her bedroom to find clothes for the afternoon. It had just gone 2 p.m.

About half-hour later, she walked into the kitchen and saw Reid standing there talking to two uniformed police officers. He was giving them instructions for the evening. Sharon knew she was going to feel like a prisoner in her own home. She would be stuck inside until tomorrow.

Reid introduced her to the officers, and then they left the house. He asked Sharon to sit down because they needed to talk before he left too. They both settled on the couch, and he took a deep sigh.

'Listen, we cannot find a Carlton Anderson anywhere that matches his description. Now the one you worked with five years ago had died twenty years ago. That is the social security number he was using. It was a stolen identity. Something very sinister is going on here, I am afraid. Looks like you have been followed for the last five years. Maybe it has been longer. We will never know until we find this guy. Now you said you drank about two glasses of wine last night.

Where is the bottle? I want to take it to forensics. Maybe you were drugged.'

Sharon was in shock. Carlton was not who he said he was. How weird was that? She worked side by side with him for a few years. How could that be? Everyone in the office knew him.

'SHARON,' shouted Reid. 'Snap out of it! Where is the wine bottle you were drinking from last night?'

'Um, I don't know. It was gone when I got up in the morning. I got the feeling that the place has been cleaned up. I could not even find my glass. It's as if nothing happened here at all.'

'Sharon, I don't know what's going on here, but I will say this. You running to the police station was the best thing you could have done. I do not even want to think about any other possibilities had you run home. I will check all your windows and doors before I leave. In addition, you have two officers outside, and tonight, there will be two more. I will call you later on to check on you. Tomorrow, I want you at the police station filling out that report. Then you are going to your sister's house. Is this clear?'

'All clear. I do not have a problem with that plan. I will call her now while you're here.'

Sharon was on the phone for two minutes and then hung up.

'She is on her way over here. I told her there is trouble, and she insists I come over to her place now. The weird thing is I did not even get a chance to tell her what has been going on. She just says to pack some clothes and she will come get me and then hangs up.'

'This is good news. Staying here tonight is not good idea anyway. We can have the officers keep watch from your sister's place. I will wait for her and make sure you're safe before I go back to the station,' said Reid.

Chapter Four

Karen Lynch

KAREN LYNCH WAS Sharon's younger sister. She was five feet nine inches tall, with emerald green eyes and copper hair. At twenty-six, she was very smart and sensible. You couldn't fool her, and she could spot a deceiver a mile off. Karen didn't understand where she got her ability from; however, she knew her special gift was like a radar detector. Karen could detect almost immediately whether a person was sincere or a phoney. Just as a counterfeit expert could quickly distinguish phoney money from the real thing, Karen with her gift of discernment could distinguish between truth and lies.

With this talent, she bore an excellent power to apply spiritual truths to daily life. Likewise with this talent, she recognised that she frequently created sound and corrected decisions and opinions. She had an insightful, intuitive mind and was able to just 'know' the truth or actuality of something by merely looking at it. Karen was also very instinctive and a take-no-prisoners type of girl.

Karen didn't just have a gift; she was additionally a well-informed and knowledgeable girl with street-smarts as well. She listened to everything that she heard before actually communicating a word. Karen's antennae would stand up whenever she felt something just wasn't quite right. She perpetually followed her first instincts. She was very astute and took a no-preposterousness approach on any given situation. She always relied on her gut instinct towards people.

Karen was running about the apartment preparing for her daily routine. She had to go downstairs to open her store. She had looked to several different locations to accommodate her retail business, and when her present location became available on the market, she grabbed it. It was a two-bedroom flat above an old carpenter shop. She knew she would be ready to convert the carpenter store into a convenience and gift store. Her father had instilled in her to make certain she saw every comings and goings in her life. She needed to have a view of all her surroundings.

There was an enormous high bay window from her living room, and she could see the street before her. Karen adored living above her store. She could see all the comings and goings. Across the road was a flower shop. She became friends with the owners, The O'Gradys. They had owned the flower shop for over twenty years. Karen's store was virtually identical, and there was a pedestrian between the two stores.

The outside of each store was a little garden and a walkway leading up to the door. She loved both stores and also the layout. The very fact she was a good friend with the O'Gradys was a bonus. With Karen's flat higher than the shop, she could see the O'Gradys store day or night. Guess you could say she was like their security built in. They had looked out for each other's business for the past five years now.

There was a road on the left side of each building, permitting her to see quite away down the street. On the right side of their store was a lake and railings encompassing that side of the building. There were a couple of boats bobbing on top of the water and one tied up near Karen's rail. Karen enjoyed sitting out there and thinking.

Running a retail business was terribly hard work, particularly, since she only had a staff of one. She preferred to keep it that way. The less headaches, the better it was for her. Karen was a buyer. She loved to buy stuff, even as a little girl. Just the texture of items and browsing over various things appealed to her.

Somebody once told her, you bought so much stuff; you should open your own store, which she did. She would travel all over the world just to find the most unusual items to put into her store. She loved to be different, and the fact there weren't any competitions for the items she sold made her store unique.

She looked at the time and realised it was getting late. 'Right, better get a move on,' she said aloud to herself. Just as she was about to rush into the bathroom, her phone rang. Karen looked at the caller ID and saw it was her sister, Sharon.

Karen grabbed the phone. 'Sharon, how are you today?' she asked.

'I am a bit shaky at the moment. There was trouble this morning, and the police are here.'

'What?' Karen shouted into the phone. 'Are you OK? No, don't answer that. I am on my way over there right now. Pack some clothes, and you're coming over here. It's safer for you to be at my place. Be ready when I get there, and you can explain everything to me then. Let the officer know you're coming here and be ready when I get there!' Karen hung up quickly so she could call Donna and the O'Gradys. Donna would have to open the store today and work it alone or at least until she could get back.

Karen was in a state of panic. She hardly ever lost her cool, but when it came to Sharon, she worried a lot. Even though Sharon was the older of the two, Father begged Karen to take care of her, at all costs. Karen didn't know for sure why, but she knew enough to know Sharon wasn't safe. Karen remembered weird incidents growing up in Bermuda.

Once at one of their favourite restaurants, The Crab's Claw, in the Crow Lane area in Bermuda, something happened Karen would never forget. What was supposed to be a fantastic family outing turned out to be anything but. The Crab's Claw still had that fifties look even today as it did back then. Karen even remembered the red booths against the wall. If she visited it today, she'd see the same red booths. The repressed memories would all come flooding back to her. It amazed Karen how Sharon didn't remember the incident when Karen asked her about it.

The family was sitting in the last booth in the diner. This was how Father liked it, always facing towards the main entrance. He liked to see his surroundings as well. Karen sat next to her father and Sharon, and their mother's back was towards everyone. Karen's legs were too short to reach the floor, so she just sat there swinging them back and forth under the table.

She was dancing her legs around to the tune in her head as she played with her doll. Her father knocked her on the leg and said, 'Keep still, Karen.'

Karen was a little embarrassed being caught and looked around to see if anyone heard her being scolded. As she scanned the room, she noticed him. This man was staring at them. Karen looked at him curiously and noticed he was actually staring at the back of Sharon's head. Karen didn't feel comfortable with the look on his face. He had a scowl on his face to the point it looked like he wanted to do harm to her. There was so much evil in his eyes. Even a seven-year-old child could recognise that look as not one anyone would want. Was Karen the only one who noticed this? She looked at her companions and saw they were deep in a conversation and oblivious to the danger in their surroundings.

Karen's eyes perused the restaurant and absorbed everyone's look or mood. She had the ability to read people. She was always able to do this. There was another family yapping away a few tables ahead of them. There was nothing unusual about that scene. Another table had a couple arguing in whispers that was so obvious by their lowered voices and determined looks on their faces.

When Karen went into one of her observation modes, she could hear all and any noises in their surroundings. Even others were unaware of some of the sounds. The sound of clinking dishes and people chattering became very loud to her. Karen heard the sound of a utensil fall on the parquet floor. It made a clang sound, and everyone in the restaurant stopped and looked towards the sound. The waitress rushed over to pick up the spoon off the floor, and people resumed their eating habits.

Karen continued to look about the room, and then she saw this other man looking at her. He had a gentle stare, and Karen didn't feel threatened by him at all. He had a full head of brown hair, brown moustache, and brown eyebrows with the most vivid bluest eyes she had ever seen. His eyes had the power to make the most aggressive soul to calm down. He stared at Karen intently, and their eyes locked.

Karen tried her best to read him, but she couldn't. She did feel like this man was trying to tell her something, but she couldn't understand what it was. Instead, she turned and looked at the evil man and spoke to her father. 'Daddy, why is that man consistently staring at Sharon?' she asked.

Martin Lynch looked at his daughter and followed her stare. The look on his face changed everything. Karen noticed the knuckles turn all white on his hands as he stared at the man. In what seemed like minutes went by was actually seconds when he whispered something to her mom. She in turn looked at this man, and you could see the fear overtake her. She gasped out loud, 'Oh my God!' Sharon continued to talk about her day and didn't seem to notice the change in her parents' demeanour. Karen noticed though. She looked at her mother and saw she wanted to cry.

The next thing she felt was her father's hand on top of her head pushing her down. *Why is Daddy shoving me under the table?* she thought. Karen was not the type of little girl who wanted to miss what was going on. She turned her head just in time to see the evil man holding a gun up to Sharon's head. Karen screamed just as her father got her under the table. She could not help herself.

Everything in the place went deathly quiet because of Karen's screams. She then noticed Sharon was under the table as well. How the hell she got there! There was a loud bang. She was sure that evil man had pulled the trigger. Karen just had to peep over the table. She could see the man with blue eyes had a grip of the evil man's arm and the gun was pointing into the air. It looked like he had forced the bullet to go up into the ceiling.

What the hell was going on? she thought to herself. She looked over at her dad and saw the look of bewilderment in his eyes.

The two men had a silent hatred in their eyes as they stared at each other. There was an unseen war of the spirits going on between the two. Sharon and Karen could hear sirens in the distance. Someone had called the police. The waitress had this gobsmacked look on her face. The girls were dying to see more of what was going on, but they could feel their parents' hands on their shoulders holding them down. What seemed like minutes passing was only seconds.

After the initial shock and gasps in the room was over, the girls were being pulled away from the restaurant in a hurry. They could finally see clearly what was happening. It was so strange how the men were still staring at each other as Karen's parents raced them past. Not a muscle or hair was moving in the place. You could hear a pin drop even over the police siren. Karen's father picked her up, and her mother picked up Sharon. They were running down the road towards their car. Her father was fumbling with his keys as they ran towards the car. She could feel his beating heart against his chest and saw the sweat pouring down his face.

She leant over to look at her mother and Sharon. They both looked very scared, and yet to this day, Sharon didn't remember the incident or whatever happened. Karen remembered a lot and kept these memories in her head, even as she grew up.

Karen got prepared quickly and ran downstairs into the shop, just in time to see Donna coming in for work. She jumped into the front seat of her car and strapped on her seat belt. As she turned the ignition on, she felt the motor come to life with a deep roar. She had purchased this car only six months ago. The 2014 Mercedes-Benz CLA-Class is the new midsize sedan with an aerodynamic design that offers the profile of a coupe with the functionality of a four door. This Mercedes-Benz sets the standard for luxury, sophistication, and technology wrapped in class.

Karen slid the Mercedes on to the street and then slammed her foot down on the accelerator, and the sports car unleashed its fury. As she raced down the street, she shot past the speed camera attached to a pole. It clocked in at eighty miles per hour.

The speed camera fitted, with sensors and radio technology quickly relayed the details to the police. The Mercedes was thundering along, leaving a line of cars in its wake.

Karen could feel herself shaking everywhere. She better hurry; she didn't want to leave Sharon unattended for too long. Father said to continually monitor or keep an extra eye on her. It seemed to her the traffic was terribly slow.

Karen slammed her foot on the accelerator. She was dodging around all the slow-moving cars. Sharon's house was like possibly one mile away. Karen knew she would get there in record speed. There was a car in front of her that was moving about twenty miles an hour. She had to get ahead of them, and the only way was to pass on the outside. She nipped over the yellow line to pass the Sunday driver. Then she noticed it. There was a parked car facing in the opposite direction, and Karen knew she was going to hit it. It all happened in slow motion, and she realised it was too perilous to try to avoid it, so she just kept going. The right side of her car struck the right side of the parked car. The sound was wrenching as the car moved along grazing it as it went. The sound was wrenching, but she just couldn't stop. Sharon needed her, so Karen kept speeding away.

The parked car's owner saw what Karen had done and raced out into the street. She flipped her phone out and took down Karen's licence. 'You bitch!' she shouted towards Karen's speeding car. Karen barely heard what the woman said. Her mind was with Sharon. Not much further to go. She unwittingly created a lot of traffic violations as she was speeding towards her destination. Then she heard the sirens and looked into her rear-view window. *Shit!* she thought to herself. 'That's all I need right now,' she said aloud.

Karen threw the gear into first and sped up even more. She was actually going to break the speed limit and try to get away from the police. She figured it might even work in her favour if they followed her to Sharon's house. Whoever this cop was at the apartment now could probably help explain the situation. She didn't care about any speeding tickets or paying for any damage she caused on the road.

Karen could actually see the turn off to Sharon's Street. She lived on a tree-lined street and had neighbours on both sides of her place. The police was not too far behind her as she slowed down. Karen pulled up in front of Sharon's door. There was a short walkway from where she parked. Karen jumped out of her car and was about to run up the walkway when someone pulled her by the arm.

'Just a minute, miss,' said a police officer. 'What's your hurry?'

She turned to confront him.

'Officer, I have just received some bad news, and I need to see my sister. She lives here,' said Karen pointing to Sharon's house.

Just then a man opened her sister's door and walked down the path towards them. He pulled out his ID and showed it to the officer. Putting his hand out to shake Karen's, he asked her, 'Karen Lynch? I am Detective Reid Sinclair. I take it you're Sharon's sister. Please go inside and be with your sister. I will handle things out here.'

Karen took his hand and shook it. Never saying a word, she flicked her head, turned, and scurried up the path to the door.

Reid felt an electric charge when he held her hand. This wasn't conventional static electricity, but more like something mystical. Touching her had awakened something deep inside him. *What the hell was that?* he thought. He dropped away the notion and moved around to speak to the policeman.

The officer informed him that Karen had ignored the officer's persistence to pull over. And to top it off, she had hit a parked car, causing destruction in her wake. There was going to be a large number of charges that she would not be able to avoid.

Chapter Five

Karen Meets Reid

SHARON AND REID had been sitting on the couch going over what had happened. Reid was still confused regarding the person in her kitchen and asked Sharon to explain him once more regarding the incident. 'You have to explain to me once again exactly what has happened and keep telling me until it makes sense,' he said. 'It just seems odd that a person would be in your house using your facilities like they had been there before. What's even stranger is that you have never seen this guy before. You might even recall something you didn't think was important.'

Sharon explained everything she could remember about him. She purposely left out the part about her wanting to die.

Fifteen minutes later, you could hear sirens screaming towards them. They heard a car screech to a halt outside her door. Reid peeped out the window and asked Sharon what type of car her sister drove. 'It's a Mercedes,' Sharon told him.

'Well, it looks like your sister is here. And she has managed to bring company.' Right behind her car was a couple of cruisers, flashing lights and all.

Reid walked out of the house and approached the officers; flashing his badge, he introduced himself. The patrol that was assigned to watch Sharon's house also got out of his car. Karen was shouting at the officers to let her pass.

Reid noticed the similarities between the two sisters. They could be twins even. He walked up to the scene and asked, 'Karen Lynch? I am Detective Reid Sinclair. Please go inside to your sister. She needs you.'

Karen could not resist the impulse to poke her tongue out at the officers. She grabbed her licence from one of them and ran into the house. Reid watched as she flew into Sharon's arms.

He stayed outside to inform the officers of the day's events for about ten more minutes before going back inside. Sharon and Karen were sitting on the couch, and Sharon was telling her the events all over again.

After Karen was informed all that had happened, she informed both of them that they were not to be separated again. It was very important that they should remain together. It was a matter of survival.

'Wait a minute. You know what's going on here?' asked Sharon.

'No, I don't know what's going on. I just know we have to remain together at all costs. Remember Dad said it to us after that man broke into our house years ago and killed a police officer.'

'Oh, shocks, yea,' said Sharon. 'I completely forgot about that.'

'How can you forget something like that, Sharon?' asked Reid.

'Easy. It was over twenty years ago.'

'Well, how is it that Karen remembers and you don't?'

Karen stood up and said, 'I remember because I talk to our parents every week, and they never let me forget. Dad reminds me all the time, always saying to keep an eye on Sharon. Sharon is fortunate. She does not talk to them as much as I do. Sharon is afraid they will try to talk us into coming home. Besides, I am more alert than she is. I am very suspicious of everyone. Too much weird stuff has been happening to the both of us. However, I must say, this is a first, having a man in the house uninvited and cooking and being chased through a park and all. Lord only knows what that was about. I do know one thing. Dad says to change your atmosphere when things seem unexplainable. Therefore, on that note, I think we should get out of here and into my apartment. It's above the store and has security throughout. It's also high up, and you can see for miles. Dad always said to live high up, but Sharon was always afraid of heights and that is why she took this place. Let's get out of here!'

'Oh, wait,' exclaimed Sharon. 'I just remembered something else. Don't ask how I forgot this one, but when I was being chased in the park, a third man showed up out of nowhere. He was chasing me as well, and I didn't see any other way out except over an iron fence. Using my gymnastic skills, I slowly manoeuvred myself over the fence, but he didn't make it over so easily.'

'What?' shouted Reid. 'You didn't mention it at the police station.'

'I know, I know, but I had Carlton on my mind. I am still shocked by Carlton.'

'OK, so what can you tell me about this third guy?' asked Reid in frustration.

'Nothing much except that he was in his fifties. I didn't have my cell with me, but there was a woman there in the crowd that gathered who took pictures of him stuck on the fence,' said Sharon.

'OK, here is what we are going to do, Karen. Take your sister to your place, and I will follow you there. Then I'll go to the police station and see if there is a report about this impaling. Go inside and stay there, and don't come out until I get back.'

Karen shook her head in agreement and grabbed up her purse. Sharon packed a few items and locked the house uptight.

Sharon woke the next morning feeling refreshed. She looked at the time glaring at the ceiling from a clock Karen had brought in Baltimore. It was 10.30 a.m. Wow! She slept late due to the fact she had tossed and turned all night. Sleep had become almost non-existent to her. So she welcomed the extra few hours in bed. For her to sleep late like this was as if her body was telling her she definitely was in need of sleep. So much had happened since the night she spotted that strange light on the floor.

She now remembered that light, and how strange it was to appear like that. She knew it was time to tell Karen about it. Karen would know exactly what to do. She would tell her sister the truth, even about wanting to end her life. She hoped Karen would believe her, as she had no one else to turn to. Reid was there, but she had not known him long enough to open up. Karen would explore all options and analyse everything that had happened until she could come up with a possible explanation.

Karen was a take-no-prisoners type of girl. She was twenty-six and smart. You couldn't fool her, and she could spot a liar a mile away. Let's just say she had a gift for that. No one could pull the wool over Karen's eyes, and Sharon respected her immensely and trusted her judgement. She would know what to do.

She climbed out of bed and went in search of her sister. There she was in her robe looking out the window. Sharon joined her and looked out. 'What you looking at?' asked Sharon. Karen looked at her sister puzzled.

'Good morning, Sharon. I am not really looking at anything. Just thinking. I hope you had a good night's sleep because I sure didn't.'

'Last night was the first time I have had a good night's sleep in a long time. Why didn't you sleep? What are you thinking about?'

'Just thinking about what happened to you yesterday. You know, nothing like that has ever happened to me. Wonder why you. Dad told me later that when we were kids, that man wanted to kill us both.'

'OK, Karen, let's go get coffee and talk about this. I need to tell you something else that happened that I didn't tell the police,' said Sharon.

'Oh no, Sharon! You must tell them everything. If you want this thing figured out, they must know.' Karen followed Sharon into the kitchen.

'I couldn't tell them this. It is embarrassing really. I am a little depressed lately and am having weird thoughts. My thoughts are about killing myself. I have been so unhappy and really don't know why.'

'Sharon! I am shocked. You would never do that. That is not your character, and you have no reason to want that. Are you low on money? Have you met a guy and did not tell me. What have you really done over there?'

'I have the money Dad sends me every month, Karen, so money is not a problem. I have not met a guy so that is not an issue. I honestly do not know why I feel like this. I am miserable, and I just want to end my life.'

Karen took a deep breath. 'OK, how often do you get these feelings? Have you actually attempted to kill yourself yet? Obviously, you do not want to die because you're still here. Something or someone changed your mind. I have always believed that people who really want to die usually does. Normally people call someone in hopes of being talked out of it. Why have you not succeeded? Did you call anyone during these depressions?'

Sharon knew Karen was going to be full of questions. She was a very thorough person. Karen was twenty-six years, but she had the mind of an older woman. She was as sharp as a whip. She had a gift for reading people and was able to spot a phoney person a mile away. Sharon respected her immensely and trusted her judgement.

'I didn't call anyone, Karen. I normally get a bottle of wine and tablets, sit at the table, and prepare myself for the event. However, I never go through with it. I normally wake the next day in my bed. Now the other night, I noticed something. I did not tell the police this because I did not want them to think I was loony. As I was about to pop my pills, to the right of me, I noticed a light on the floor.

'It was the weirdest light I have ever seen. It had rainbow colours swirling and twirling around on the floor. I was not sure if I was drunk or just plain crazy. But the light started to take form. I decided to run, but paralysis came over me. I could not help but stare at it. I tried to reach out, but then there was this voice. It spoke to me in a very loud voice. DO NOT MOVE. After I blinked a few times, I could see it was a man. He was standing there looking at me. Then my chest started to burn, and I could not breathe.

'The next thing I remember is waking the next morning covered in bruises and nothing else. I could not tell Reid this. He would not have helped me. That's it. You're the only person I have told.'

She breathed a sigh of relief and felt much better getting that off her chest.

Karen had been listening to her intently. She finally stood up and started pacing. I knew she was figuring out this in her mind. She finally spun around and said, 'First, let's get one thing cleared up. I do not think you are suicidal. I think that somehow someone is putting the thoughts in your head. Someone wants you dead. Maybe it is in the wine. I do not know, but that is not your thoughts. This I am sure.

'Second, we need to call Reid and take a visit back to your place. We need to find that bottle of wine, and you can show me where this light was. I am wondering if the man in the robe is the same man frying eggs the next morning. We don't have to tell Reid about the suicide part, but we can tell him our suspicions about the wine.'

'He already suspects something about that wine because he asked me for the bottle, and we couldn't find it. He thinks maybe I was drugged and that is why I cannot remember anything.'

'OK, we still got to get over there. Give the place a good looking over. You said the guy cooking had the frying pan in his hands. Let's get that pan. We need prints. Maybe he used the bathroom and did not flush. He has to leave something behind if he was there all night. Do you remember what he looked like? Describe him in every detail you can.'

Sharon beamed at her sister. She threw her arms around her. She just knew Karen was the sensible one. She was always one step ahead. Karen always said, 'There is an explanation for everything.'

'OK, from what I can remember he was dressed in a colourful robe. Kind of like a religious outfit. I could see jeans poking out under the robe. His skin colour was a bit light colour like he was American Indian. Or maybe he was of mixed race or lived in the tropics somewhere. He definitely was a mixed breed, maybe Mallotta. His long hair was brushed back into a ponytail. The more I think about it, the more I remember he was the same man who I thought I had brought home from a bar the night before.'

'Hmm, you're not the type of person to bring home a guy. So I'd say you definitely didn't have a one-night stand,' Karen told her. 'I will cancel any plans I have and spend more time with you. I have to call the store and make arrangements for the next few days. I will be spending as much time as possible with you. I do not want us to separate. We have to keep the alarms on in here at all times. OK! I mean it, Sharon. Do not stray away from me. Remember, Dad said that's important.'

'Don't worry, Karen. I am not letting you out of my sight. I might have to get some Velcro and stick us together. Should we call the folks and tell them what's going on?'

'Sharon, they already know and are on their way to Miami. They do not want us coming to Bermuda as that is where the very first incident took place. In case you're wondering, I did not call them, Reid did. He wanted his hands on the police reports from before. It was Mom who said they will come and bring the reports with them.'

Sharon called Reid and asked him if he'd take them back to her apartment.

'But why? The men chasing you might still be there lurking about.'

'I have a few things I need that I didn't get last night. Also, Karen wants to see the place up close. She is like a detective. The girl studies everything.'

'OK. I have a few things to finish up here. Then I will pick you both up. I don't want Karen driving. She is like a maniac on the road. After that, you both have to go to airport to meet your parents. I can drop you off there, and you all can catch a taxi back. Don't worry, you have detail, and they will be watching out for your safety. Only trust the hat strokers.'

'Hat strokers?'

'Yes. They are the guys who let you know they are there by stroking their hats. A cap, beanie, or hat, anything on top of their head. They generally run their fingers along the rim to acknowledge their presence. If you see that, then he is your detail.'

'What if I mistake someone else for a hat stroker?'

'Just ask Karen her feelings about it. If she is as good as you say, she'd know who to trust.'

'Point taken.'

'I will be there in about an hour.'

'OK, see you then.'

Sharon and Karen chatted about all possibilities as they got ready to go to her place. They were dressed and ready when Reid arrived around 10 a.m. He stood at the door and looked like he had no intentions to come inside. He was dressed in jeans and T-shirt. There was a hole in his jeans around the knee, ripped look, just like he liked it. You wouldn't think he was a cop if you didn't know him.

'Why you dressed like that?' Karen asked him. 'Are you undercover or something? I don't think I'd want to be seen with you dressed like that!'

'What's wrong with the way I look? I have you know, this is the only way to look normal in our business. Do you think I should be in uniform? Or worst still, a suit and tie looking so obvious? Police don't do that any more. Only the assigned units wear a uniform. Now let's go!'

Chapter Six

Karen Gets Shot

THE THREE OF them arrived at Sharon's house at twelve noon. The first thing they noticed was one of her neighbours running up to the car. She wasn't a small woman and wasn't in shape and found herself almost out of breath. Sharon jumped out of the car and saw the look on her neighbour's face. She trotted over to her to save her a few steps.

'What's wrong, Alice?' asked Sharon.

Between gulps of air, Alice struggled to tell her.

'There has been a man studying your house all morning. He is gone now, but I have been watching. It looks like every twenty minutes or so. If he keeps to schedule, he will be back in, let's say', looking at her watch, 'in another six or seven minutes.'

Sharon looked at Reid and silently asked him what their next move should be.

Reid asked Alice, 'Can we come to your home? We merely want to find out who this man is.'

'Yes, yes,' said Alice, 'I'll make lemonade,' and she walked briskly back to her house.

'You two go over to Alice's house. I will move the car in front of her house. Ask Alice if she has any clippers or lawnmower or something and to bring it to me in the yard. Go, move, move, quick.'

Sharon settled on the couch peeping out the window by pulling the curtains slightly across. No one could see her looking out, she was sure. Karen joined her on the couch and threw the curtains all the way back.

'Don't do that, Karen. He will see us.'

'No, he won't. He won't even be facing this direction. Also, it's in the afternoon. If he looks this way, he will only be looking at a dark window. Act like it's an ordinary day.'

It was never going to be an ordinary day. Nothing had been ordinary since she woke yesterday morning. There had been a man in her house, men chased her in the park, and men tried to kill her as a kid. Nothing was ordinary. Tears threatened to well up in her eyes. She knew she was starting to cry, and Karen knew it as well. Karen shimmered closer beside her sister and wrapped her into her arms. Sharon kept blinking her eyes, hoping the tears would turn back to her eye sockets.

'Let it out. Allow it all to come out. It's a great way to relieve stress. It really is going to be all right. As long as we are together, we will sort out this whole mess. This I promise you. When you feel like giving up, remember why you held on for so long in the first place.'

Sharon was sobbing on her sister's shoulder. She was relieved she had a wonderful sister. She had always been there for her, always willing to take on all Sharon's troubles as if it was hers.

Alice walked into the room with a tray of beverages. Sharon brushed her hair with her hands when she saw Alice enter. She hated anyone to see her cry.

'Here you go,' said Alice. 'A nice glass of lemonade is what you need, my dear.'

'Alice, I think the police officer in your yard wants some grass clippers or something to make it look like he is cutting your grass. He wants a good look at that gentleman. It's best you go and see what you can help him with.'

'Oh, I see. My ex-husband left an old beat-up mower in the garage. I will get that out for him. It's the push type so it should be able to work. Unless it needs oiling,' she laughed, running off to get the mower.

Sharon and Karen sat on the couch looking out the window, watching and waiting. Not long after, they saw a car pull into the cul-de-sac. They watched as the car drove along the roadway and past Alice's house. They could see

Alice walk up to Reid and say something to him. Reid started to take pictures of the car, and the man didn't even notice, for he was so intent on looking towards Sharon's house. Five pairs of eyes were slowly following this man's movement, watching as he drove past.

Karen got a little frustrated with the whole scene and got up off the couch.

'It's time someone asks this man what the hell he wants!' exclaimed Karen. She walked towards the front door and opened it.

'Karen, don't! Let Reid handle this,' shouted Sharon.

'No. You just cannot leave things up to the police. They drag it out too long. I want answers now.'

And with that, she stormed out the door and down the walkway towards Sharon's house. The driver of the car had reached the end of the cul-de-sac and was on his way back down the road towards Karen. Karen had walked right in front the car with her hands on her hips, looking directly at him as he approached.

Everyone was stunned at her brazenness, but not a soul moved. Reid looked towards Alice's house, but he could not see Sharon in the window. *What on earth is she doing?* he thought to himself. He and Alice stood watching as the man pulled up alongside Karen, and she walked right up to his window.

'You seem a bit lost, sir. May I help you?'

'No, I don't think so. I am looking for a friend.'

'Well, it seems to me that you're looking for your friend for a while now. Every twenty minutes it seems. Maybe I know your friend. What's the name of this person?'

'Sharon Lynch. She lives here somewhere.'

'Well, I am Sharon, and I live in that house you keep staring at. What can I do for you, mister?'

'You're Sharon?'
'I am indeed. Now I won't ask you again, what do you want with me?'

The man got out of his car and stood next to her.

'So, you're Sharon. How do I know for sure you are whom you say?'

'Listen you, I don't even know who you are. You said you were looking for your friend and that I am that person. What do you want with me? I don't have time to play games with you.'

He stood back and reached inside his pants, pulling out a gun. Karen gasped and turned to run back, but it was too late. She could hear someone scream out her name.

The man heard the name 'Karen', but it was far too late. He had aimed his gun at her and pulled the trigger. There was nothing anyone could do to prevent the bullet from hitting her. He looked towards the man who had called out and knew instantly it was a cop. He jumped back into his car and took off down the road.

Reid had watched the man intently taking pictures as he did so. He was astonished to see Karen walk out of the house and confront the guy. Reid knew it wasn't going to turn out good when the guy got out of his car. Not taking his eyes off the two people talking, he rested the camera down on the lawnmower and told Alice to go inside. Then he saw the bulge under the guy's jacket, and he knew what it was. When the man reached for his gun, Reid shouted out Karen's name. But it was too late. He ran towards the two of them with his police radio up to his lips. He could see the man jump into the car, so Reid ran to his own car and went chasing after him. You could hear him shouting into his radio and advising the operator there was a shooting at 842 Pearle Avenue.

In the distance, Karen could hear Sharon screaming or was it Alice's screams. Karen felt the pain in her arm as her legs buckled underneath her. She was going down. It felt like slow motion to her. Was this a dream? No, because she felt the warm blood trickle down her arm. She fell to her knees, scraping them as she did so. She could smell the gunpowder in the smoke from his weapon. Sharon was running out of the house and directly to Karen. Alice ran into the house to call the police and ambulance.

'Karen, Karen, are you OK?' shouted Sharon shakily. Her heart was beating so fast; she thought it would explode. She knelt beside her sister and held her by the shoulders.

'I am fine. Did you see that? That jerk shot me! Oh, all the nerve. I am so mad right now. I have been shot! He made me scrape my knees too!'

'Karen, why, oh why, did you confront that man? You just couldn't leave it to Reid, could you? What on earth were you thinking? Life is too short to be taking these risks.'

'What do you mean life is too short? It's the longest thing anyone can do. Once you die, that's it! There is nothing else longer than that,' exclaimed Karen.

Sharon helped her to pull up off the ground, holding her arm as she did this.

'Karen, you're not understanding. I was scared to death. I thought he was going to kill you.'

'It's just a flesh wound. His aim is as lousy as his breath. Besides, if you had died of fright, then he would have accomplished his deed. You see the thing is he thought I was you. So you are the one who he was looking to kill. When he heard someone shout out my name, it startled him. It startled me too. We were both taken off guard. This is why he missed.'

'You're so funny at times, Karen, but now isn't one of those times I find you funny. Let's just get you inside while we wait for the ambulance. Alice, can you stay here and let the ambulance know where we are?'

'Sure, Sharon. I might just need that ambulance after this. I nearly died too. I felt my breakfast coming up in my throat. You people sure know how to jump-start an old gal's heart.'

They walked into Sharon's house, and Sharon got a towel and wrapped it around her arm to help stop the bleeding.

By the time Reid returned, the ambulance attendants had seen to Karen. Her arm was properly bandaged, and she was acting like nothing had happened. Refusing to go to the hospital, she instead wanted to look over Sharon's house.

When he walked into the house, both women looked at him, waiting to hear if the guy got caught or not. 'I lost him,' Reid informed them. 'He is a professional I believe. But I do have his licence tags and a picture. We will get him for sure.'

Sharon asked, 'How did he not kill Karen if he is a professional?'

'I can tell you that, Sharon,' said Karen. 'Reid startled him when he called my name. We both got startled. I'd say you saved my neck out there, Reid.'

'I'd like to wring your neck! Why did you come out of the house? I had it under control. This was a great opportunity for the police to find out more information. Now that he has escaped, we may never know what he was up to,' exclaimed Reid.

'I know what he was up to. He wanted to kill my sister is what!'

'Karen, you must tell me the extent of your conversation with that man,' Reid demanded of her.

'I only asked him if he was lost. He said no. He claimed he was looking for his friend. I asked him who his friend was, and he said Sharon Lynch. I told him I was she, and that's when he pulled out his gun.'

Looking over at Sharon, he said, 'So we can safely say, he was trying to kill Sharon.'

'Yup, somebody wants my sister dead.' Karen also looked over at Sharon.

Sharon felt both pairs of eyes on her. They made her feel uneasy. She did not like that feeling. 'Listen, guys, I don't know why anyone wants me dead. I honestly don't. I am

sure Mom and Dad could fill us all in when they get here.'
With that, she got up of the couch but felt a sharp pain rush
through her. She fell over on the floor in a foetal position,
holding her stomach. Karen and Reid both rushed over to
her aid.

'Sharon, what's wrong?' asked her sister.

'Not sure, just got this terrible cramp all of a sudden. I
have had this cramp before, and it soon passes. Let's just give
it a minute. It will pass.'

Reid picked her up off the floor and laid her on the
couch.

'Have you eaten or drunk anything since you've been
here?'

'Nope, haven't eaten a thing. Just had coffee at your house
this morning. I have not been in the mood to eat. But these
cramps are not unusual. I have been getting them frequently
lately. I'll just drink a little water. I have bottled water in my
bag.'

'OK. You rest here. I am going to look about your place.'

Sharon watched as Karen and Reid walked about her
house. She closed her eyes and cleared her mind and allowed
the calmness to wash over her. It was a glorious feeling to
have someone near her whom she trusted. They would have
to go to airport soon to meet her parents, and Sharon wanted
a clear head when they arrived.

Meanwhile, Karen and Reid moved about the place looking for clues. They just couldn't find anything. They were in her bedroom and noticed the bed. It still looked like it hadn't been slept in. Her clothes were still thrown about as she had been looking for things to pack to take with her to Karen's place. It was just difficult to decide where to start. They could hear Sharon fidgeting on the couch so Karen wanted to hurry out of there.

'OK, Reid, why don't we do this? You comb the kitchen and living room. I'll do the bedroom and bathroom. We can get through this more quickly so we can take Sharon back to my place.'

'Great idea, Karen. You're not just quick to jump in front of bullets, but you're also quick in your thinking as well.' He couldn't help but chuckle.

She didn't find him funny. 'You just removed any doubt I had about you being foolish. You should have kept your mouth close. Let's just do this. I am feeling creepy here and don't know why. It seems like someone is looking at me.'

Reid huffed off to the kitchen. That Karen was unbearable. He didn't know why, but she got to him. Maybe he was just still irritated with her for confronting that guy with the gun. She was the silly one, confronting that guy like that. *Oh, well,* thought Reid, *let's see what we have here.* Looking about the kitchen, he noticed the frying pan the guy had used. He used a paper towel and picked it up and placed it in a paper bag. He also bagged the utensils and anything else he thought that guy might have touched. The kettle, toaster, and even the knobs of the stove were added to the collection. He would send the entire bag to the lab for analysis. He searched in the fridge and cabinets and drawers. There was nothing. There were two plates, two forks, and two cups on the island. One set had been used. Sharon did mention she ate the eggs after the man had left. So he took the unused plate for the lab as well.

Off now he went to the living room. Sharon was still lying on the couch, but she was tossing and turning. He wondered what was going on in her head at this moment. Never in all his years had he seen a potential victim went through so much. His determination to protect her was somehow pressing to him. He didn't know why, but he would do his best to protect her. There was an inner voice in his head telling him that these girls needed him, including Karen, who could be a nincompoop at times. That girl knew how to get under his skin. Reid walked to the bar.

'Hmm,' he said, 'what an unusual bar. Very nice.'

'What did you say?' asked Karen. He turned to see her standing there looking at him.

'Sorry, I didn't realise I had spoken out loud. I was actually talking to myself. Just admiring the bar is all.'

'It is a lovely bar, isn't it? I believe it was special made to Sharon's specifics. There is a secret compartment somewhere. I have seen Sharon run her fingers along the base there, and a door clicks open. It's her most expensive wine. No one gets to drink from them bottles.'

'Is that right? Let's see now. This might be interesting.'

Reid ran his fingers along the base until he felt a bump in the texture. He pressed and heard a click, and the secret door flipped open.

'Sweet. I like this. So how did you make out in the bathroom and bedroom?'

'Nothing. I found absolutely nothing. Her bed doesn't even look like it's been slept on in days. Wonder what she has been doing over here on her own. Sulking in self-pity I bet. I should have been visiting her more often.'

'Why self-pity? Is she depressed or something. Maybe a boyfriend is what your sister needs, someone for company.'

Karen wouldn't dare tell him about the suicidal thoughts, even though Karen felt those thoughts were somehow placed in her sister's head. The only cause was someone wanted her dead. If she had killed herself, that would have saved someone else from doing it.

'Maybe I shouldn't have said self-pity. Maybe more loneliness is what I mean. Guess, I feel a little guilty for not coming over more. She doesn't drive, so she doesn't visit me. She runs everywhere. It's like she keeps her body holy, never dated. Never done the things girls of our age normally does. I haven't even seen her watch television.'

'Wow. How do your parents feel about that?'

'Oh, they are very protective. I know they are hiding something. It's strange with all these people trying to kill her and my parents treat her like she is fragile. I really don't understand it. Talking about my parents, we better go pick them up at the airport.'

Reid looked at his watch. 'Yes. It's getting that time. I wasn't going to go with you to the airport, but since you're stunt today, I better stick with you both. How does your arm feel?'

'It's a scratch. Barely felt it breeze by me. I have had worst injuries than this. Believe me.'

'I am afraid to ask. Promise me you won't do anything stupid like that again.'

'I must admit, that was stupid. If I knew ahead of time that that fool would shoot me, I would not have confronted him. For that I am sorry.'

'Promise me you won't do it again. If you break a promise, then sorry means absolutely nothing because promises mean everything.'

'I promise. Lord knows I don't want to be shot again.'

Sharon heard their whole conversation. 'I am your witness, Reid. I heard her promise,' she smiled.

They both turned and looked at Sharon sitting up on the couch.

'You're up. How are you feeling?' asked Karen.

'Much better. Thanks. I needed that rest. How did you guys make out? Find anything?'

'I got all your utensils from the kitchen. I am going to send it to the lab for forensics. There has to be some kind of trace left by the guy,' informed Reid.

'Well, let's go to the airport. We want to be there before the plane lands.'

Reid put the things in the back of his car and helped the girls get settled in. He looked about the neighbourhood to make sure no one was lurking about. He didn't notice the shadow by the trees across the street. It was the same shadow of the man by the same tree who was watching Carlton the previous day.

They drove off to the airport to pick up the Lynches. Reid couldn't wait to get his hand on the police reports from Bermuda.

Chapter Seven

The Lynches Arrived from Bermuda

THEY DROVE TO Miami International Airport in silence. They each indulged in their own thoughts during the drive. Sharon was thinking about her parents. She had not seen them for over a year now. It was going to be great to see them. Reid was thinking about the police reports. He just felt that the answers he needed were in there somehow.

Karen's mind was all over the place. This was so typical of her. She was trying to digest everything that had happened and solve the riddles before anyone else could. That was the competitive side in her. And how was she ever going to tell her father that she failed him. He specifically asked her to keep an eye on Sharon, but Karen was too busy running her store to check on Sharon. If only her parents would tell her what was really going on. Well, she was determined to shake it out of them on this visit.

There they were, waiting in the busy terminal. It was like a zoo in there. Karen decided to go sit in those uncomfortable blue chairs and wait while Reid and Sharon went to check the arrivals board. She could sense the excitement of the holiday-goers, waiting to be flown to their vacation destination; however, Karen couldn't share in their excitement, for she knew she was going to get a scolding, especially for being shot.

Karen needed a cocktail. As she looked around for the nearest bar, she saw Reid walking quickly towards her. Then she noticed he was literally dragging Sharon by the arm. He deposited her next to Karen and said, 'Stay here, in sight. I cannot be sure, but I think I just have seen that man who shot you. He must have followed us here.' Reid was on his phone in a heartbeat.

'We can go to the bar for a cocktail.'

'No, stay right here. Someone is coming in five minutes to be with you while I look for your parents. Don't move, and I mean it, Karen!'

'How on earth could you have someone here in five minutes? That's simply not possible.' Karen was sulking as she wanted that drink.

'They have been with you since yesterday. I told you. You have detail. But because they are hidden, your killers may think you're alone. It's time I bring them out in the open. I don't want to take any more chances.'

Joined by two plain-clothes police officers, they all walked in a line formation to the arrivals gate to meet the Lynches. Reid was leading, then Karen, then Sharon, and the two police officers were following in the rear. Miraculously, Martin and Christene were the third people to exit the door.

Immediately, you could see the years have grown on them. Martin's hair on the side of his head had whitened. Christene had white streaks running through her long black hair. She had such beautiful olive skin. She had not had one wrinkle on her face, but you could ascertain her age by other means. Christene was a beautiful woman indeed. To say the apple didn't fall far from the tree was putting it mildly. The girls looked like their mother. The older couple complemented each other when they walked side by side. People would turn their head to admire them. They were what one would call a match made in heaven.

Upon seeing their parents, both girls started to shed tears. It was so wonderful seeing them. Sharon flew into her mother's arms, hugging her tightly. Karen was holding back just a little bit and was happy to wait for her turn. She knew they were worried about her with people trying to kill her.

Hugging her father, she exclaimed, 'Dad, it's so good to see you. Hope you had a pleasant flight!'

'It was pleasant enough. We were anxious to get here. Your mother has been very worried about Sharon.'

Reid stepped forward and put his hand out to Martin. 'Sir, I am Detective Reid Sinclair. I have been working on your daughter's case. Sharon is fine. It's Karen you should be worried about. She got herself shot not long ago.'

He reached over to shake Christene's hand, but her hands flew up to her mouth.

'What!' she shouted. She took Karen by the arm and looked at her.

'It's fine, Mom. It was a flesh wound. The bullet barely touched me. Detective here is overreacting,' Karen told her while looking at Reid and rolling her eyes.

'The thing is, madam, it could have been worst. But let's get you out of here. I don't like standing around. There have been some strange occurrences. Did you bring the police reports?' Reid was all business.

'Yes, we brought them, and I agree, I don't like being here either. We are all going to Karen's place. I like it better there as we are high up,' instructed Martin, picking up his case and walking off. They all had no choice but to follow him. It was clear he was in charge of this group.

The drive from the airport was uneventful, but Reid knew they weren't alone. He had used his flashing police lights so they could get back to the store quickly. The sooner they were inside, the better he felt.

There were a lot of people milling about around the store between the gift store and the flower shop across the road. There was other business in the area, but only these were close by each other. The two plain-clothes officers stayed outside the store, smoking and chatting. Reid wanted the killers to know they had their work cut out for them if they wanted to kill Sharon.

Karen had gotten her parents settled in the spare bedroom before they went into the kitchen to make tea. Martin and Reid were out on the back verandah, sitting by the water. There were only two police reports that Martin had given him. Reid had read them and was questioning Martin about the incidents. 'So this guy, Danny McGregor, he was shot dead at the scene. Can you tell me a little more about him?'

'I only know what the reports say. Except that I found out a few weeks later that he was married with kids and came from Indiana. He never checked in a hotel and had a return ticket for the next flight out. He had no police records. He had never been in trouble that the police could find. He didn't comply with the officers' demands and threatened them so they shot him dead.'

'Shot him dead. Hmm, I was told a long time ago that Bermuda had a firearm law. No guns were allowed there.'

'This is very true. Only under certain circumstances such as sporting events like competitive shooting are they allowed. You have to have a special licence. If there is a sporting event, participating athletes apply well in advance to import their firearms under a temporary licence. Those with a licence are not allowed to have their gun in their home. They are confiscated and held at the regiment until the day of the sport. The Bermuda Regiment and the Bermuda Police Force are authorised to hold a Bermuda licence firearm. However, not all members carry a gun, only a special branch of the force.'

'I wouldn't mind living down there. Not a day goes by here without a shooting.'

'I don't think you would want to live there if you like open spaces. Bermuda is one of the smallest places in the world. Compared to the United States 9.629 million kilometres, it's only fifty-three square kilometres.'

'Well, I wouldn't mind that too much. Living on an island sounds grand to me. I'd own a boat and be out on sea every day. A nice tan I'd have as well,' smiled Reid.

'You can get that right here in Miami. Not too many differences with the weather.'

'Well, here it takes me over an hour each day to get to and from work. In Bermuda, it would take me ten minutes, correct?'

'Well, that would depend, if you lived in the middle of the island, maybe it would take you less than ten.'

'Exactly. I hate all this driving. I may even get a moped. Now that's right up my alley.'

'You will also be the owner of the famous Bermuda road rash. There isn't one person who hasn't experienced that,' laughed Martin.

Both of them were laughing when there was a tremendous crash coming from inside the kitchen. Martin and Reid both jumped up and ran into the apartment. Karen, Christene, and Sharon were all standing there looking down at a tray of mess on the floor.

'What happened?' asked Martin. 'You give us a fright. Is everything OK?'

'Sharon dropped the tray is all. Nothing to get excited about,' said Christene.

'Wait a minute, Sharon, are you OK?' It was Karen who noticed Sharon was not in a normal state of mind.

They all looked over at Sharon, and they could see she was in some sort of daze. Christene rushed to her and put her arms around her shoulders.

'Come, Sharon. Come sit down,' she said. 'What has happened? Did you get hurt?'

Sharon looked up at all of them and said in a matter-of-fact voice, 'He was here.'

Reid shouted in his radio, alerting everyone to be on the lookout. Karen ran about the apartment, looking in each bedroom. She then called downstairs to Donna and checked up on the store.

'People are coming in and out all day, Miss Lynch. We have had a few good sales but nothing much else happening here. I do want to go out for a bit in like thirty minutes, though, if that's OK. What was that crashing sound? Gave me the jumps.'

'My sister dropped a tray. When you're ready to go out, just let me know you're going and lock up the stop. You can leave for the day. I'll come down later and ring off the register.'

'OK, I'll see you tomorrow then. I'll be here at 9 a.m.'

Karen returned to the couch and sat beside Sharon. 'I don't understand, Sharon. I looked through the whole place, and no one is here. No one is downstairs who doesn't have a right to be there. Explain exactly what happened.'

Reid chided in, 'The men have circled the property. There are no suspicious people outside either.'

'OK, I had just finished mixing the drinks and was taking them to Mom and Karen when I saw him. He was standing there looking at me. It was the same man from my apartment. I wasn't frightened by his presence, but he startled me, and I dropped the tray. Mom and Karen rushed up to me, but he was gone. That's it. I got the feeling he was trying to say something to me, but his mouth wasn't moving.'

Christene walked up to Sharon. 'Sharon, is it possible you was hallucinating or something? Where did he go, honey?'

'That's just it, Mom. He didn't go anywhere. He is still here. I cannot explain why we don't see him now, but he is still here. I feel it in my bones.'

'We cannot go by a feeling. We need facts. Sharon, you have had a lot happen in the last forty-eight hours. Maybe you just need some rest,' exclaimed Reid.

'No, Reid, Sharon is right. I feel like we are all being watched. I have had this creepy feeling now since Sharon first called and told me what's been going on. There is something more spiritual or mystical happening here. I think Mom and Dad have to tell us what's going on here.'

Looking at her parents, she said, 'I think you both know more than what you have been telling. It's time you come clean. We are adults now. Not those scared little girls any more.'

Martin and Christene looked at each other. Their unspoken words confirmed what Karen was saying. Martin sat in the armchair and looked quizzically at Christene. 'You can tell them what we know, honey. It's about time they knew the truth.'

Christene got up and walked to the window and looked out at the people below. She was trying to find the words to begin. Then she settled on asking Reid a question.

'Do you believe in angels, Mr Sinclair?' she asked.

'Angels? Um, I never really gave that a thought. Do they exist you mean? I don't know, and I don't know if I will ever believe they do,' he replied.

'Let me tell you. They do exist. Angels are benevolent celestial beings who act as intermediaries between heaven and earth. While they are messengers of God, they are also protectors of humans. Each and every one of us has our own angel protector. We just don't know how to communicate with them. They try to communicate with us while we sleep.' Christene took a deep breath and continued, 'Certain angels have developed unique personalities and roles, which make them archangels. These angels are ranked among the good angels mentioned in the Bible. They will battle satan and satan's army in the end times. But in the mean time, God has sent them to earth to prepare us all for the end times. Some angels have taken on the role of a human and walk amongst us but are in actuality Nephilims. Nephilims were born to the archangels and humans. It was a way for the archangels to communicate with the humans, through their offsprings. We have all been assigned our own angel, and they are with us every day.'

'Mom, what are you saying exactly?' asked Karen.

Christene sighed, 'A long time ago, when you were a few days old and Sharon about thirteen months, I got a visit. I was still in the hospital, and your dad was at home babysitting Sharon. It seemed like a dream. He didn't walk through the door. He just appeared. He said things to me. I couldn't move. I just sat there and let everything he said be absorbed into my mind. He informed me that although I bore you both, you and your sister was only on loan. We had been chosen to care for you and to bring you up. He said Sharon had a destiny to fulfil and you, Karen, you was her protector. Of course, I didn't believe this, and I thought I had had a bad dream. But when Martin came to visit the hospital, he told me he had a weird experience. He had a dream that someone visited him and told him our girls were "special". This occurred at the same time as my dream. We couldn't believe we both had the same dream at the same time. It was very weird for us.'

'OK, Christene, your story is getting creepy,' said Reid.

'Well, Mr Sinclair, things got ever weirder over the years. As the girl grew, they had strange accidents that would have killed any other child. However, I was always alerted somehow about their distress and was able to save them.'

'Give me one example,' requested Reid.

'Well, there was this one time, Karen was squealing my name, even though she barely could speak. I came running to find plastic wrapped around Sharon's head. She was gasping for air. The wrap was so tight that I had a hard time getting it off her. There was no one else in the room except Karen, who was in her crib. If the police had been called, they would have arrested me for sure for attempted murder as no one else was in the house. It was later when Martin and I were talking about the incident that I realised Karen had spoken. I could swear she called out my name as loud as she could. But when we looked at her, she was playing and cooing as any baby would be. It was always something happening though. And it always seemed to be Sharon almost dying. We were at our wits' end. We soon came to except what that man had told us, which was we MUST protect her at all cause and that Karen would always know what to do.'

'Has Karen always known what to do?'

'Yes. She always directly or indirectly had saved Sharon, for instance the shooting. It was meant to be that way. Only Lord knows what would have happened if she didn't go out there and get shot. That drew the attention of the whole neighbourhood, didn't it? In spite of your belief, Mr Sinclair, she has done the right thing. It was Karen who saved us all in a restaurant once. She told Martin a strange man was looking at us, and immediately, we knew we were in trouble. But that other man was there too, the one who visited us.'

'Dad, what does this man look like?' asked Sharon. 'The one who visited you at night and told you we were special.'

'Well, he sorted looked Indian, American Indian. He had long hair in a ponytail. That's all I can say about him. I never see facial description?'

'Sounds like the man in my place frying eggs the other day. It's the same man here today. I wonder who he is. He actually talked to me in my kitchen. He actually cooked at the stove. I sure wish I hadn't been so hasty in throwing him out the house.'

'It's OK, Sharon. You didn't know. If you're the only one who he can communicate with, he will be back. Just trust in the Lord.'

'Mom, I feel like my life is under construction. I never knew why I didn't have any goals like Karen. She wanted her own business and went for it. She wanted a car, and when she was able, she got it. I never even wanted to drive let alone own a car. And while we are at it, I might as well tell you. All I wanted to do is die, and almost died too by my own hands.'

'What are you saying, Sharon?' shouted Martin while standing up.

'You might as well know. I was attempting to kill myself a few times by taking pills and alcohol. But every time I tried, I'd wake the next day not remembering what happened. Just that I'd wake bruised as if I had been in a fight or something. It was that way the other night when I woke and that man was in the house. I just cannot remember what had happened.'

'Oh my God, Sharon, what if you had succeed?' Martin was beside himself.

'Calm down, Dad. I don't think she tried to do it. I think someone has been drugging her. Maybe a mind-altering drug that would make her do this. But I think this man, whoever he is, was always there to stop it. I am the one you should be scolding. I wasn't there to protect her,' Karen said very disappointed with herself.

'Wait, you all made my head spin. Angels, mysterious man in your dreams, suicide, I mean come one now. Am I supposed to believe in all this hocus-pocus stuff?' asked Reid.

Everyone turned and looked at Reid. They all knew it was a lot to digest. Even for them it seemed hard to believe.

'Let's just take a break. Sharon, you go get some rest. I think I need to lay down myself. I can understand Mr Sinclair having a problem with what he's heard here today.'

'OK, Mom. I am going downstairs to do some business, and I have to think,' declared Karen.

Reid decided to go back out to the balcony and read the police reports again. 'I will read the reports again, just in case I missed something important.' And with that, he strutted off.

'Guess I'll check in at the station. There will always be cops about even if you don't see them, so don't worry. I will be back. Besides, you have your guardian angel,' he said sarcastically walking out the door.

The room seemed to clear instantly. Everyone had something to do. Sharon went to lie in Karen's bed to rest as her mother was in the spare room. Her parents' visit had exhausted her, and it wasn't long before she was in a deep sleep.

Sharon was lying in bed sound asleep until there was an inner voice prompting her to open her eyes. She opened them very slowly. Before her was this vision levitating at the foot end of her bed. The vision had a very light green mist surrounding it by a white mist. Inside this mist was the form of a human man. It took her eyes a moment to adjust before she could fully see it. Fear gripped over her when she couldn't identify what it was.

She opened her mouth to scream, but nothing would come out. Silence. She tried to sit up but could not move. Total paralysis had sent it. This was one of her scariest moments in her life. She was sure this was a visit from beyond. *Beyond what?* she thought. *Maybe, possibly a world unknown to her yet.* All she could do was lie there and watch this apparition levitate above her bed. Soon there was a calmness surrounding her, and she was scared no more. She came to terms with her vision, embracing it even.

A peace came over her as a light rolled over her body. Different colour lights illuminated around her. She had to smile, for she felt happiness and peace. Then there was this voice, talking to her, telling her to not be afraid. This voice had told her she needed to go to this building. It didn't say what building, but instead, it placed the image of the building in her head. After the information was transmitted to her, the apparition slowly dissipated into thin air until the last drop of mist was gone. It was then and only then could she move.

Chapter Eight

Marcus Sherry

MARCUS SHERRY WORKED as a freelance self-employed electrician. He was twenty-eight years old and knew it was time to settle down. He wanted kids before he was thirty-five. He wanted to be able to do things with them before he was too old to move.

The guys he worked with were always trying to set him up with a girl. Nothing ever materialised with these dates, except maybe a second date that ended in bed. He dated this one young lady whom he enjoyed being with. He met Kim through one of the blind dates his mates set him up with. She was truly exciting to be around. She could be a bit flighty at times, but she made him laugh. Kim loved wearing red, and anything she had on had to be in red. The thing was, though, she simply had far too much red going on around her. He could see her coming from a mile away. Once when he had visited her apartment, he noticed red clothes all over the place. She even had bright red curtains up to every window in the place. Kim was always chirpy and smiling though. She was a lovely height for him and had gorgeous red hair. No wonder she loved red.

One night, they were lying around his apartment relaxing and watching television. It was very quiet in the room, and it appeared as if they both were engrossed in watching TV; however, they both had things on their minds. He picked up on this and turned his head to look at her only to catch her staring at him with this curious look on her face. This had surprised him, and he wondered what the hell she was thinking. Then she rose up off the couch and scooped down on her knees in front of him. Marcus's mind immediately went into the gutter. He thought she was about to perform a fellatio act on him. Call him old fashion but he was a strong believer in safe sex and would not agree to cunnilingus in any form. That should be between a man and a wife. That was a fallacious assumption, however. She took his hands in hers and said, 'We have been hanging out for a while now, and I really like you. I think we should be thinking about getting married.'

Marcus's eyes grew as big as saucers. He was shocked to say the least. He couldn't believe what he was hearing. He started to think about how long he had known this girl. She really liked him, she said. Shouldn't a couple be in love to be discussing marriage? 'Hanging out' was another term she used.

Shouldn't they be doing more things together than 'hanging out' in an apartment? Dinner, movies, going for walks holding hands were just a few things people in love do. Besides, he wanted to do the asking when the time was right. He had a perfect marriage proposal planned for that special day. This definitely wasn't the beginning of a long-term relationship he had in mind. He didn't want his future wife to be sleeping with him so soon after meeting each other.

This was not the way he wanted his wife to be. She had to say no to him for at least five dates or more. Besides, he wanted to find his own permanent girlfriend, not someone that was found for him. He didn't want to wear that label that he wasn't able to find his own woman.

Someone who asked you to marry them was someone who loved you. If you didn't want to marry that person, no matter how you sugar-coat your answer it was going to hurt them.

'This is a wonderful surprise from such a wonderful person. You have caught me off guard. I would never have imagined that you were thinking along the lines of marriage. I will need to say no because I am not ready for marriage yet.' This was all he could think to say. She was not impressed with him after that day, and the visits fizzled. He now no longer saw her at all.

He was now ready for marriage and wanted to take on a wife.

Marcus liked to go to the laundry mat to see if there were any possible matches for him, but most women there had tons of children's clothes. Going to church wasn't an option, and the nightclubs were out of the question. He didn't mind going to the clubs, but he didn't want to meet his future wife there. His preferences were to see her in the daytime where no alcohol was involved.

Possibly he could see her in the park or at a job site he operated on. He was deep in thought as he walked along Biscayne Boulevard Way. He really wasn't paying attention where he was going when he looked across the street and then he saw her. What a beautiful vision for his eyes! She was about five feet eight tall. She had long dark brown hair. She was very plain looking, but she had God-given beauty. That was one woman who didn't need make-up.

Marcus was admiring Sharon. He imagined her in his kitchen fixing his dinner. He was dreaming about all the possibilities of a relationship with her that he didn't notice she was looking back at him. *What beautiful eyes,* he thought to himself.

Snap out of it, Marcus. Staring is no way to impress a girl, he said to himself.

He flashed his grandest smile, raising his eyebrows, and tipped his cap to let her know he was interested. He waited to receive her confirmation for his flirt, but instead, he noticed a sigh of relief on her face. She started walking towards him.

Goodness, Marcus, he thought to himself. *You've got it going on to be able to attract a woman as beautiful as her.*

He fidgeted as he stood there. *What will I say to her? Marcus, calm down!* She was almost upon him. As she approached, he practised what he might say, not once even considering a simple hello. His mind was racing.

She walked right up to him and said, 'Good day. I understand you're here to protect me. There is a man following me. I am just walking about discovering Miami. I might go to Bernie's restaurant on Miami Avenue. You can come there after you get rid of them. I will only be there for about an hour as I have to meet Karen. Thanks.' And then she walked off, looking behind her every two seconds.

Marcus looked around and saw no one following her. Everyone seemed to be in hurry, but not one person was going in the direction she went.

'Hmm,' he hummed to himself. Of all the women in this world, he flirted with a nutcase. He watched her slip into a fertility clinic and rolled his eyes. He decided to forget about her and looked around for another possible suitor. He was about to give up when a man approached him. This guy looked like Will Smith in *Men in Black*. He wore dark suit and dark glasses. He was tall, with a blank look on his face.

'Excuse me, sir. Good day. A young lady was just here talking to you. My wife. I seemed to have lost her. Did she mention where she was going?'

Instantly, alarm bells started to ring in Marcus's head. He was not sure if the bells were because he felt guilty flirting with another man's wife or if the woman was telling the truth. He decided to play it safe and lie. If this man was her husband, he could catch up with her later at home. On the other hand, if he was following her, then he would have done his good deed for the day by protecting her. That's exactly what she said too! That he was there to protect her. Besides, if this man saw her talking to me, then surely he saw which way she went, he thought.

'Oh, you mean the lady with brown hair? She asked me for directions to the train station.' Marcus nodded his head, pointing with his chin in the opposite direction where she had gone. 'She went that way.' With that said, Marcus turned and walked away with not a glance behind him.

Now which way should I go? he thought to himself. He wanted to follow the beautiful girl but didn't want to go that way, in case the man was watching him.

He decided to go to the jewellery store next to the clinic. That way, he could watch from inside the store what was going on. He stopped to look at some of the items in the window. Pretending he was interested in the items, then turned and went inside. Once he was inside, he casually looked out of the window, and yes, that man was looking in his direction. *Why was he looking at me?* he wondered. A young lady came up to him and asked if he needed assistance. Well, he might as well try on a few watches. He did need a new one after all. He wanted to spend at least thirty minutes in there, even though this wasn't where he wanted to be.

Marcus stayed in the jewellery store until he could see the man eventually walked off. He watched to make sure he disappeared from his sight.

With a new watch on his arm, he left the store and walked in the direction Sharon went. He knew she was in that clinic, and he decided to go in there too.

Sharon had woken to a quiet apartment and didn't see anyone around. She still was very confused about what was going on. There were so much unanswered questions. Why had she been suicidal? Why after all these years Carlton had showed up? She now believed that that running into him in the park was not an accident. She knew for sure, he had been there by design. How long had Carlton been watching her? Why were men trying to kill her? Why was Karen shot?

Sharon dressed quickly and went in search of her sister. Karen wasn't anywhere to be found. Sharon looked for a note or something to indicate where Karen was, but there weren't any visible notes anywhere. She peeped her head out the front door. It was a hot and humid day outside, and the birds were chirping. *This means no rain today,* she thought. Against all advice and with what had happened with Karen being shot, Sharon decided to go for a walk. A walk would do her good. Besides, she knew that out there somewhere, her police escort was not far. She just needed this time to breathe in the air and think about all the recent events. She decided to take a small towel with her because it was one of those days that even the best dressed wouldn't be able to hide the sweat staining their clothes.

She glanced down the street and noticed no one was looking in her direction. No one was even looking suspicious or looking at the apartment. People were buzzing about minding their own business, dripping in sweat. Sharon knew, had they bothered to look at her, they'd see, her body would look the same to them—all sweaty and sticky. Children were playing oblivious of the heat. Children always seemed immune to the layers of heat. They simply loved it and didn't break a sweat.

The heat was so intense, so energy absorbing, that Sharon wouldn't have the energy to run if she needed to. She decided to take bottled water with her. The trees had summer's full bloom of leaves, and not a leaf moving. There was no breeze to disturb the sun's relentless, burning attack. The bright blue sky lay in the humid air, with no clouds to be seen. The heat bounced off the streets and caused a mirage of wavering images. A dog stood by with its tongue hanging out in an effort to keep cool.

She decided to go a walk to town and back. It was only about a mile away, and she could use the exercise.

Sharon was in deep thought as she walked along the town sidewalk. There was something nagging at her. Her inner conscience was telling her to look across the street. She could see a man looking at her. She wasn't sure what to do, so she just stared back at him. She now noticed he saw her looking at him, and he slightly nodded his head and tipped his cap. *Oh*, she thought to herself, this must be one of Reid's men assigned to protect me. She decided to go over to him and let him know where she was heading.

After informing the man where she was going, she continued on her way enjoying her walk. A few minutes later, she saw a building that was extra white and clean. This building was sitting between two taller buildings that clearly needed work. Odd. Why was it that was the only building on this street that looked taken care off? Sharon decided to satisfy her curiosity and walked across the street to get a closer look. As she got closer, she noticed a small sign above the door that read Fertility Clinic. Odd again. *Why is there a fertility clinic sitting between two decapitated buildings?* she thought to herself. She didn't fight the urge to go inside to take a peep.

There were no windows on the building, but there were indentations where a window used to be and looked recently plastered over. Sharon reached out and placed her hand over the doorknob. For some odd reason, her hand was shaking. Anticipation ran through her whole body. There was something or someone on the other side of the door waiting for her. She just felt it. Whatever was behind this door had been waiting for her for a while. She looked behind her to see if anyone saw her going inside. Good, no one she recognised saw her entering.

Once inside, she quickly closed the door behind her. There was nothing unusual about the inside. The normal expected scene as in a doctor's office waiting area. A woman sitting behind the counter looked up as Sharon walked in. 'May I help you?' she questioned. Sharon ignored the question and couldn't hide the irritation with the woman. Obviously, this receptionist wasn't busy. She stood there and looked around, absorbing her surroundings. There were three doors behind the reception area. Two of the doors were adjacent to both side of the receptions/nurse and one door in the centre.

There were posters all over the walls about sperm or female eggs. There was another poster about the reproductive system. On either side of the room was a couch and coffee tables. Both coffee tables had egg-shaped glass top with six sperm-shaped legs holding up the glass top. *What unusual tables*, Sharon thought.

Again, the receptionists asked, 'Madam, may I help you?' Sharon turned and looked at her, as if seeing her for the first time. The woman was immaculately dressed. All her hair was piled on top of her head with a few loose strands dangling down her face. She stared at Sharon intently as Sharon walked towards her.

'I am not sure if you could help me or not. I was walking along the street, and somehow, I was drawn here. Something about this place caught my attention. Is this a fertility clinic?'

'As a matter of fact it is! But not just any ordinary clinic, we serve special clients with appointments only. Maybe pure curiosity brought you inside, but if you don't have an appointment, then you have to leave.'

'Maybe I would like to make an appointment.'

Just then the door opened and in walked the man she saw on the street, the man she believed to be from the police department. She gave him the biggest smile he had ever seen.

'Give me one moment,' Sharon told the receptionist and walked up to Marcus.

'Hello again,' she said to him stretching out her hand.

Marcus eagerly took her hand and shook it.

'Hello. Sorry, if you think I am following you, but I just wanted to let you know there was a man outside looking for you saying he was your husband.'

Marcus saw the fear take over her face.

'I am not married, and I am afraid if a man is out there looking for me. It's not good that he finds me.'

'You said earlier, you thought I was your protector. What did you mean?'

'Are you not from the police?'

'No. My name is Marcus Sherry. I just happened to notice you and admired you from a distance.'

'Oh my. Oh, Lord. Oh, goodness,' was all she could say.

'Listen, I am sorry you thought I was someone else. I was merely flirting I guess. In any event, this guy, something about him gave me the creeps. I sent him to the train station when he asked where you went. He must have seen us talking.'

'OK, I am going to have to break up this reunion,' the receptionist told them. 'You cannot stay here.'

Just then, simultaneously two doors opened. The main door opened and in walked the man who was looking for Sharon. The door to the left of the reception also opened and out came a man in a white coat.

'Oh, good, Miss Lynch, you're here for your appointment. You and your boyfriend can come this way,' said the man in the white coat, holding the door open for them to enter. Marcus and Sharon looked at each other. They then looked at the receptionist. Her composure had not changed, and the revelations from the doctor didn't surprise her either. She simply said, 'Move along now. We have another client.' Turning to the man who walked into the room, she said, 'Good day, sir, do you have an appointment?'

Marcus and Sharon didn't wait to hear his answer. They quickly followed the man inside. They were led through another door, where he locked it behind them.

'Listen, I know this may sound strange to you, Miss Lynch. But you're in serious danger. We have to get you out of here.'

'You know me?' Sharon asked incredulously.

'Yes. I was watching you walk along the road. I have been your guardian for most of your life. I cannot explain it all to you now because time is of the essence. I had been waiting for when you was strong enough to give you this.' He reached inside the drawer and pulled out a thick envelope. 'Here, take this with you. All you need to know, you will find inside this envelope. There is a back way out of this building.'

Marcus was stunned by what he was witnessing. *What on earth did I get myself involved in?* He now wished he had gone the other way.

Suddenly, there was a thud on the door. There was the sound of fighting. Sharon looked towards the door and could actually see the vibrations of someone being thrown up against the door. The man rushed up to a very large bookcase and pulled it towards them. It was a door. There was a long hallway visible. 'Quickly now go inside and follow the hall all the way till you see a red door. Go through that door, and it will let you out on Palm Avenue. Marcus, stay with her and make sure she gets back to her sister's house safely.'

Marcus realised this strange man called him by his name. The longer he stayed here, the more he wished he were somewhere else. Marcus didn't let on that he was scared. The sound of breaking glass filled them both with dread. Sharon grabbed the envelope and headed for the bookcase's secret door.

Suddenly, the noise stopped. They heard a key in the door. All three of them looked towards the office door and saw the receptionists standing there. Her hair was no longer piled on top of her head. She was a shambles, but somehow, she was able to retain her composure. She gave a nod to the man, and he seemed to relax a little.

'Sorry, sir,' she said. 'I just knocked him out a little bit. He will come shortly. This will give you a fifteen minute head start.' She walked over to Sharon and gave her a giant hug, saying, 'I am sorry about earlier, Miss Lynch. I didn't realise it was you. I am honoured to be in your presence. Please forgive me. Whenever you need something, I will always be here to serve you.'

With that said, she turned and walked out the room, locking the door behind her. Sharon was still in awe and didn't know what to say. She just turned and walked down the hall. 'Come on, Marcus, let's go.'

Marcus looked at the man and nodded his head before following Sharon down the hall. He stopped and looked back and noticed the man had closed the bookcase back. It was a blank wall, not a sign of a door ever having being there. *Weird,* he thought. He rushed to catch up with Sharon.

'What's going on here?' he asked.

'I haven't a clue,' she replied.

'Aren't you curious? Gosh, there really is a man following you. Just like you said outside. Why is he following you? Who are these people? What is going on here?' Marcus pulled her by the arm, making her to stop and look at him.

With a deep sigh, she said, 'All I know is, someone wants me dead. I have been chased, shot at numerous times over the years, and possibly poisoned. And when my sister finds out I left the house, she will definitely kill me herself. I just want to get back home before she finds out. Will you escort me there?'

There was a sound from whence they came so he said, 'OK, OK. Let's get you home. I know how to lose a person if we get followed.'

With that, they went off in search of the red door. Marcus scurried down the long corridor trying to keep up with Sharon.

Chapter Nine

MARCUS HAD TAKEN her through all the backstreets, walking quickly and dipping in out of stores looking behind them. There was no one he could see following them, but he didn't want to take any chances. He felt pressure on his back, pushing him to make sure he saw her home safely.

Finally, they came upon a taxi stand, and he jumped in it pulling her beside him. It was then and only then, he felt he could relax a little. He didn't want to reveal to her how frightened he was. They pulled up in front of a store, and Sharon told him, 'We are here. This is my sister's store, and she lives above it. We will have to use the side door to get in. It looks like the store is closed for the day.'

She knew she could trust him. It was his eyes that gave away his trusting nature. She didn't have any reservations about taking him upstairs to meet the family.

'I'll wait here. You go and inform them about my presence. I'll hang out down here to make sure no one followed. Don't want to give anyone any surprises like I had today.'

Sharon agreed and put her key in the door. As she walked into the door, everyone rushed towards her. They were so concerned.

'Where have you been? We have been frantic. You promised to not leave my sight!' shouted Karen. She was incandescent with fury.

'Calm down. When I woke, no one was around. I went for a walk. I knew I wasn't alone so I felt safe. Besides, where was everyone? You all left me!' Sharon threw her envelope on the counter and placed her hands on her hips.

'Did you think to look on the verandah? We were out there waiting for you to wake up. You're lucky I didn't call the army to look for you.'

'Well, there was someone following me. I thought it was the detail Reid assigned to me. However, I was able to allude him, but not without the help of Marcus.'

'Who is Marcus?' asked Christene.

'Oh, I ran into him by mistake. He helped me get back safely. He is actually outside. I thought I confront the storm in here before I brought him inside,' informed Sharon.

Martin looked at his daughter incredulously. 'I cannot believe you brought a stranger here after all that's happened!'

'His name is Marcus, Dad, and if he wanted to kill be, I'd be dead by now. I had been with him alone for the past an hour now. He actually helped me. If it wasn't for him, I just might be dead. Now let me go get him, and you can meet him.'

'No. I will go. You stay here and beg for forgiveness from your mother and sister,' Martin said, walking to the door that led down the side of the building.

'I am going to call Reid and check in with him. I thought he would be back by now,' said Karen.

Martin stood on the landing looking down but didn't see anyone. He decided to go to the bottom of the stairs and looked around the corner. He saw a man standing there whistling, and he called out to him, 'Are you Marcus? Come this way.'

Marcus turned and saw a distinguishable gentleman looking and gesturing towards him. He was about to walk over to him when all of a sudden out of the darkness came another man.

He grabbed hold of Martin and pulled him away from the door, causing the door to close. It was then that Marcus saw a blade in the mysterious man's hand, and he jumped into action. He ran over and grabbed on the guy by his arm, spinning him around and catching him off guard. Marcus had used such force that the knife went flying to the ground. This man was no more than thirty years old, with unshaven face and dark circles under his eyes. He looked like he had not slept in a long time. Marcus rolled up his fist and lashed out and gave the guy a wallop beneath his chin. Martin could do nothing but watched. He pressed himself up against the wall so as not to get in the way. Martin knew his fighting days were over and couldn't offer assistance.

Wow, Marcus thought to himself, *how on earth was I able to do that?*

The man had fallen to the ground stunned, but aware. He touched his lips and looked at his hand. He was bleeding, and this angered him. He rose up of the ground and charged at Marcus, but Marcus was too quick for him, and he gave him another punch that threw the guy in the air and he landed with a thump. It was lights out for him.

Just then, two other men came running up to them with guns drawn. Martin was sure they were the police who had been watching the house.

'Where have you guys been? I was attacked, and thanks to this man, he knocked the guy out.'

'Sorry, sir, we know what happened. We had been watching. We were running a check on the guy who saved you. Congratulations, Mr Sherry. Looks like you bagged a bad guy.'

Marcus was not impressed and stayed silent. A smart man knew when to stay silent while the police demonstrated their ignorance. They were probably sleeping or something he thought.

'Darn it,' Martin said out loud. 'I don't have a key to get back in.' Just as he said that, Karen opened the door. She looked at the scene before her and knew immediately her father had a close call. 'What's happened? You didn't come right back so I got worried.'

Marcus introduced himself and said, 'The guy on the ground pulled a knife. I had been standing right here and didn't see him until it was too late. Don't know where he even came from. He would have had to pass me, but he didn't.'

'Well, I for one would like to thank you for saving my life,' said Martin, holding out his hand to shake Marcus's hand. 'He certainly took me off guard. Come upstairs for a stiff drink. Lord knows I could use one.'

'Um, no thanks. I think I better get home. I have had enough excitement for one day. I have a feeling it's not good for my health to hang around here.' Passing Martin a card, he said, 'Here, take my card. If you need me for anything, my numbers on there.' Marcus passed his card to the police officers as well. While tipping his hat towards Karen, he said, 'Madam' and strutted off down the road.

The police put cuffs on the perpetrator and called it in. Karen could hear Reid's voice boom over the radio. 'I'm on my way back there. Hold him there before you take him in. I want a chat with this fellow.'

In the mean time, Marcus was walking down the road in deep thoughts. How and why did he allow himself get caught up in whatever was going on? He could not help but think about Sharon. She was a beautiful woman, and he found himself attracted to her in a fierce way. He second-guessed himself and wished he did go upstairs with her father if just to absorb her beauty one more time. He was so engrossed in his thoughts that he didn't see the misty shadow following him. He looked at his watch and realised time had passed by quickly. He decided to walk all the way back home. It would be dark soon, and he was hungry. He imagined dinner at a nice restaurant with Sharon sitting across from him.

Marcus got a weird feeling he was being watched. *Oh gosh,* he thought, *someone else is following me now.* He believed it was one of Sharon's followers. He didn't have a cellphone on himself so he just decided to walk quicker. There was traffic passing by and people around so he wasn't too concerned. He just didn't like the feeling of being watched or tailed. He stopped and looked behind but could not see anyone out of the ordinary. He ran across the road to the other side so he could jog against the traffic. He never liked cars behind him when he jogged, always preferred to face them head-on. He wasn't running fast, but he did pick up speed with his jogging. However, he still couldn't shake the feeling he was being tailed. He could see a McDonald's restaurant about 200 yards up ahead and decided to make a dash for it there.

He was almost about fifty yards away when the hairs stood up on his neck. Whoever was following him was no more than six feet from behind him. He stopped and turned to look, and then he saw him. This shadowy figure stood there looking at him. There was a glow about him. A peaceful glow surrounded this figure, and Marcus was not afraid no more.

He stood there and watched, and the glow got closer to him. He couldn't run even if he wanted to, for it was upon him. The mist surrounded Marcus and enveloped him inside.

He felt strange things happening to his insides. Something was pulling on and squeezing his guts. *What is happening to me?* he wondered. He tried to look around to see if anyone saw what was happening to him, but he could not move. Soon, he could feel himself rise up above the ground. There was nothing under his feet. He was floating. Where did the ground go? He could feel his body turning and turning in slow motion circles. While looking straight ahead, he could see the face of a man. This man had a wonderful look on his face, and Marcus wasn't scared at all. He looked into his eyes as the mist surrounded them, and information filled his brain.

Then slowly he felt his body moving downwards until his feet touched the ground. Marcus had this sudden urge to pee. The misty glow slowly left him and floated away. Marcus stood there looking at it as it disappeared into the air. The mobility returned, and he could now move. He jolted around and looked towards McDonald's.

There a woman stood, watching him. Maybe she saw what he saw. He walked up to the woman and asked her, 'Did you see that?' She did not reply to him so his eyes followed hers and noticed she was looking at the puddle of liquid on the ground by his feet. He then realised his bodily fluids had escaped him, and he had not even felt it. Embarrassment rose up to his cheeks, and he turned beet red. All he could do was run. He ran towards his home and never looked back.

Chapter Ten

Adonai

SHARON LAY IN bed thinking. She really wanted to know what this was all about. Was this her destiny? Was this her purpose for being? Everyone had wondered at some time in their life why they were here on earth. What was the significance of her life or her existence? Why was she put here? She did not want to be one of those who speculate, but there had to be answers somewhere. Was there any value to life? It had been much speculation from a scientific point of view, but she felt it was more a symbolic reason that she was here. She just needed to figure it out. There should be a reason for everything.

She stared into the darkness as she thought about all these things. *What will be my fate?* she wondered. Then she remembered the envelope. She left it on the counter. Sharon had to study the papers. She was promised that she would understand more about her destiny. Sharon got out of bed to go get it and read. The apartment was in darkness except for a night light in the small hall. As she turned into the living room, she could see Karen sitting on the couch with a light illuminating beside her. She was reading the papers.

She looked up and saw Sharon enter the room. 'Hello, there, Sis, you cannot sleep?'

'Nope. I cannot. I have so much questions in my head,' revealed Sharon.

'How's Dad?'

'They are both sound asleep. Thank God for your friend who saved Dad. He seemed like a nice enough guy. What sort of questions you are asking yourself?'

'Well, Karen, you ever wonder why you're here? Who designed you? Who or what makes you tick? Why is your heart beating and there is no battery to keep it running? Why is there so much activity in our brains? Who feeds us our thoughts? Those kind of questions I am asking myself.'

'There are lot of questions and a lot to think about. Maybe all your answers are in the Bible. I for one have been reading your papers, and there is a lot of information here. Where did you get this information?'

'That's why I got up. I just remembered the papers. I came upon a clinic today when I went for a walk. I don't know why I was drawn to that clinic, but I went inside.'

Sharon relayed all that had happened during her walk. She had no clue who this man was, and this was the first time ever she had seen this clinic, even thought she had travelled to the town in the past. Karen agreed; she never saw a clinic in the town either.

'Once the man had given me the papers, Marcus and I were told to go out through the back door. We could hear fighting going on as we walked down the hall, but we didn't stay around to find out what happened after that. Then Marcus saw me here. I forgot I even had the papers till just now.'

Karen rose up off the couch. 'Well, I have been reading your papers. Remember when Mom and Dad were talking about angels.'

'Yea, I remember. They said angels are all around us.'

'What they didn't tell you was that that you were an angel, not a full angel but a Nephilim. You are the angel of Adonai and a human.'

'Who is Adonai?'

'Adonai is connected to God and is ownership of our lives. I suggest you read Genesis 18: 3 to learn more about Adonai. It will also show you the revelation of the future and intercession.'

'So you're saying, I am part angel and part human? What about Mom and Dad? They are both human and responsible for my presence, Karen.'

'Yes, but it seems they were used as a vessel only. We are all children of God, and we are all connected.'

'So then, it's God who put us all here. How is Adonai connected?'

'The name of God that we know it in today's understanding means Lord or Master of all. Adonai is a name known or used back in the beginning times.'

'So God is Adonai. Then it is he who is responsible for me.'

'Yes, he is the one to whom you submit or bow down to. He is the boss of your life. Adonai is the ultimate authority figure in your life and the one whom you owe your complete allegiance. Here is what your papers say:

'Adonai has the power to be everywhere. He watches and waits. What is he waiting for? Well, he needs you, his prize creation, to complete a task that he had set out for you.'

Sharon stood and walked along the room thinking. Then she remembered the visit she had while she slept. She remembered what she learnt during that visit. This was the way he planned it. He needed her to fulfil a task without any pre-knowledge so as the deed would be done without any judgements or pre-notions. He created her. She carried his blood. She had to be strong, for she was his angel. She would carry out the will of Adonai, with the power and guidance of the Holy Spirit. This was her destiny. She turned to Karen and said, 'I understand it all now. It's flooding in my brain as we speak.'

She was the pathway for all angels, no matter what form that an angel came. Real angels would always point the way to Adonai. Angels were not the replacements of the transcendent God. They were the servants of the transcendent God and would always serve him.

They were the Redeemer of humanity, with complete willingness, and she would do his will. There would be forces out there trying to hinder her, but Adonai would not let anyone come in her way. He would protect her, for he also had his forces out there, watching over her and guiding her. His forces didn't even know the reasons for their willingness to help her.

Sharon was a modern-day angel. In time, she would accept this, for he could not intervene in her transformation. She would need to get in touch with her inner angelic person to realise what and who she was. This would allow her 'wings' to grow. She was an angel in training.

Once her wings had grown and she knew her destiny, she would no longer be a she. For all angels were genderless. She would no longer be human. She would no longer have the feelings as a human. She would no longer have the desires of a human. A modern-day angel was of value to today's society. Modern-day angels also told us that the new future was near. So much closer than any human could possibly think.

'Karen, I think I will take these papers inside and read them more in-depth. Thank you so much for being the best sister in the whole world.' Giving Karen a hug, she walked off into the bedroom.

'Good night, Sharon. Sleep tight' was all Karen could say. She had her own thoughts to sort out.

Once back in bed, Sharon got comfortable by curling up to read all the information. She knew Karen was going to sleep on the couch so she would be able to read without disturbances. After reading for about an hour, she noticed a movement from the peripheral of her eyes. She turned to look to see what it was, thinking Karen or her mom was checking on her. But to her horror, it was a black creature with dark wings flapping and staring at her. Its red eyes stared at her with pure hatred oozing from its eyes. The creature soon noticed she had seen it. This prompted the creature to move closer to her, and Sharon was about to scream, but nothing would come out.

She could not move. The creature was in control of her. It walked closer to her, and the closer it got, the bigger it seemed to become. Suddenly, it jumped on top of the bed and leant over her. She caught a whiff of the most putrid smell as it snarled and growled at her. She was able to see its feet, looked more like claws, digging and digging into the mattress.

It clung to the mattress so tightly; the tips of its claws disappeared inside the bed. It reached out for her, stretching its arm over to her neck. About a millimetre of an inch away, a bright light loomed over the black figure. The creature jerked around to see the brightest white light hovering over it. Sharon saw it too. Clear as day, a giant angel emitted from the light, and the dark figure shrunk back smaller to its original size. There was no mistaken in its own fear, for it knew the powers upon them was far greater than his own.

Sharon was able to move and jumped up off the bed and ran for the door. She stopped suddenly and turned to look back into the room. The creature was gone, and there standing in the corner was the man from her house. He just stood there staring at her. She was scared no more and walked back towards the bed. Neither of them had to speak words, for she was in full understanding of who he was now. He informed her telepathically that she would be OK and he would not leave her side. They talked this way for another two hours, and Sharon finally went off to sleep. Her angel sat on the bed beside her for the rest of the night.

Early the next morning, Sharon woke to voices coming from the kitchen. It was her sister, her parents, and Reid. She walked out of the room in her pyjamas and said, 'Good morning.' They all were sitting around the table with papers thrown all over the table. Everyone turned and stared at her, and not one of them said morning back to her. They had shocked, astonished looks over their faces.

'What? Why you all looking at me like that? I will change my clothes later, but for now, I just need food.'

It was Christene who rose up and walked to her daughter.

'Sharon, my dear, have you seen yourself? Please, let's go look in the mirror.'

Sharon followed her mother and looked in the mirror in the hall. She was slightly frightened to look for everyone's faces told her she might not like what she would find. She slowly turned towards the mirror and looked into it. There standing before her was a young lady with, not the dark hair she once knew, a full head of totally wavy white hair and additional bruises around her neck.

She stared at the image not recognising herself, but she knew it was she. She had accepted this vision, for she had no choice.

She walked back into the room and informed everyone there, 'I had a visitor last night. I saw who or what wants me dead. It was the most ugly, vile creature ever on the face of this earth. This is the same creature that tried to kill me before in my house.'

'Oh my goodness, Sharon,' exclaimed her mother.

'It's all right, Mom. I understand everything more clearly now that I have read the contents of that envelope. I have also been informed on what's happening, and I now know how to deal with it and what it is I have to do. You see, Adonai was there too. He saved me from that evil thing in the room.'

'Who is this Adonai?' asked Reid.

'I will let Karen bring you all up to speed with that, and you're welcome to read the contents of the envelope as well. That would give you a better understanding.'

'I was about to tell them when you came into the room,' said Karen.

'What exactly do you have to do?' asked Reid.

'Well, first thing I need to do is find a vial. I believe it's at that clinic Marcus and I was at yesterday. I need to go there and get it. I don't know exactly where it is, but I do know it's there. There was this woman there. She will help me get what I am looking for. After that, I need to go to Ireland and find this mountain. It's called Croagh Patrick Mountains and found in the county Mayo. We may need to speak to an orographist. I need to understand this mountain, for I am told I must walk up that hill until I reach the top far beyond where any one man has gone before.'

'What's an orographist?' Martin showed his confusion.

'It's a person who studies the top of mountains. This includes the hills and the elevated terrain of the mountain as well as what grows on the top or even the weather changes up there. I will need to know all this information before I can go up there.'

'Why is this so important?'

'Well, I am told I will know more as time goes on. It's learning as you go type of task. When I get there, I will know what to do, for I won't be alone.'

'No, you won't,' said Karen. 'Wherever you go, I go too. Don't try to take me out of it. I am going with you.'

The buzzer went off to the door downstairs. Someone was here so early. Reid rose from his chair and looked out the bay window. He could just about see the top of a man's head.

'Can you come over here, Karen, and identify this guy at the door?'

Looking out of the window, she told Reid, 'It's the guy who saved Dad yesterday and helped Sharon get back home. His name is Marcus. Marcus Sherry I believe.'

'Hmm, OK, I will go down and let him in.'

Karen believed Marcus just wanted to size him up closer before he was allowed inside the apartment.

Sharon was telling her parents and Karen what else was expected of her when Marcus and Reid walked back into the room, just in time to hear her say 'It's his will.'

'Whose will?' asked Reid.

Karen spoke up, 'I can answer that question, Reid. It's God's will that Sharon complete a mission that he has mapped out for her. It's her destiny. Sharon and I have done some research last night, and we have discovered that Sharon is a Nephilim. She has been put on this earth to carry out a task that only an angel could. We are all here to help her see it through and make sure she gets to where she needs to be.' She turned to Marcus and said, 'This includes you as well, Marcus. We are all here to help her. I read a lot last night, and that's what I can conclude from the papers.'

Marcus stood up. 'Listen, something happened to me last night. I realise I just come into the picture, but when I left here yesterday, a presence came to me on the street. Literally picked me up off the ground and spun me around and round, communicating with me through my mind. It told me to be here this morning, and I would discover what it is I am supposed to do. So here I am.'

Marcus wasn't about to tell them he was so scared that he relieved himself right there in front of McDonald's.

'OK,' said Reid. 'Let's all go over the last few days and then decide what we are going to do. We still have to try to protect Sharon until we can get to Ireland. There are men out there who will try to stop her from doing whatever she is supposed to be doing. The best defence is offence. First, we compile everything we know so far. Then we can go from there.'

'I agree,' said Karen. 'Here's what I know and think. Someone has been trying to poison Sharon. How and when they did this, I am not sure, but I believe it's in the water at her place. It's some kind of mind-altering drug that's forcing her to drink wine and take pills. Whoever did this knows it's God's ultimate sin and wanted to relish in their success if Sharon carried it out.'

'Yes, that would be great power for whoever has done that. But Adonai saved me every time. I didn't know it then, but I know it now. I have been attacked in the middle of the night as well. That's how I get the bruises. It's some kind of entity that attacks me. Last night, I have seen it for the first time and remembered it. My mind is so clear now,' said Sharon.

Karen continued from there, 'The man in your house was Adonai. He showed up just in time to save you. He has always been with you. Him cooking breakfast the next morning was the first time he showed himself in human form.'

'Now that explains why I cannot find any fingerprints on all the stuff I took from your house. I did get the reports from Bermuda, and the guy who tried to kill you as little girls is Danny McGregor. We don't know the connection, but we can tell you he was an everyday guy. He didn't have a police record or any run-ins with the law. The police officer who handled the case in Bermuda says, Danny did whisper in his ear that the girls must die. They cannot offer anything else to help us find out who is behind all this,' Marcus informed everyone.

'Then you're chased in the park by Carlton Walsh and an unknown assailant. I do have a picture of both of them chasing Sharon in the car park. Hopefully, something will turn up soon. We cannot track them down anywhere though. It's as if they didn't exist. Also, the guy who was impaled on the fence in the park is in the hospital. He is a mystery as well, and he isn't talking, just sitting on his bed looking into space. The police are at the hospital right now guarding his door. And then there is the guy who shot you, Karen. I spent most of the night going over mugshots to see if I could find him. Nothing. Another one who doesn't exist.'

Christene stood up and declared, 'I'll get on the phone and see about flights to Ireland. When do we all leave?'

'Mom, you and Dad are not going. Just Reid, Karen, Marcus, and myself are the only ones going to Ireland. That's it,' said Sharon with determination.

'Sharon, it's my homeland. I am not missing an opportunity to go home. Besides, we have to make sure you get to the right mountain. No one knows Ireland like I do. Now that's finale. We are going,' Martin told them all.

Sharon knew she would not be able to change her father's mind. Once it's made up, that was it. She might as well get used to that idea. Karen was nodding her head in agreement, so it looked like six people would be travelling to Ireland in search of the Nephin Mountain.

Marcus said nothing about him being included in this trip, for he wanted to go with them. His urge to travel there was great, and he knew not why.

'OK then, here is what we are going to do. Christene, you and Martin make all the arrangements needed for the trip. Arrange for a private van to be waiting at Ireland West Airport Knock. Make sure we have six cellphones as well,' instructed Reid.

'Wait, I have a friend Michael from Ireland living right here in Miami. I am going to give him a call. Next to Dad, he knows Ireland, and I believe he is from County Mayo,' said Sharon.

'Do you trust him, Sharon? If you do, give him a call. See what information he could help us with.'

'I trust him with my life as I trust everyone in this room.'

'Karen, I think you and I should go to this clinic Marcus and Sharon were at. I don't think you should go there again, Sharon. Karen and I can get that vial you speak of.'

'OK, Reid, but I also want to go to the hospital and talk to this guy. I have a feeling I might be able to get something out of him,' informed Karen.

'Oh, you a cop now. You think you can interview this guy?'

'Yes, as a matter of fact I do. Police do everything wrong when they want information.'

'Is that right?'

'That's absolutely right. I am sure I can get something out of him. I cannot put my finger on it, but there is something not quite right about him. Please let me go see him. Then we can go to the clinic after.'

'OK, Karen, you win. I'll take you over to see him, but you're not going to be in his room alone. Marcus, can you stay with Sharon and help her with whatever she needs?'

'I will indeed. That's what I was told to do yesterday when I was floating in the air, to not let her out of my sight.'

'OK then. Everyone knows what they have to do. It's going to be a long day. Karen, get ready so we can get an early start.'

All of a sudden, there was a large thud on the roof. Everyone froze. It sounded like something fell on the roof. Reid instinctively took his gun out of his holster. He wasn't taking any chances. They all went to the bay window in the living area, looking out and waiting for another sound. But nothing came. Karen took up her binoculars and searched the surrounding area. 'Where are your guys, Reid? I don't see anyone.'

So then Reid called on his radio to see if the guys were out there.

Reid: 'Hey Joe, this is Reid, you there?'
Joe: '10-4. I am here.'
Reid: 'We heard a noise. Do you see anything?'

Joe: 'Negative.'

Reid: 'Well, what do you see?'

Joe: 'I see you all looking out the window.'

Reid: 'Are the other guys in position?'

Joe: 'Affirmative. I am looking at them too.'

Reid: 'We heard a noise on the roof. Look up there.'

Joe: 'Negative. Reid. I don't see anything.'

Reid: 'There definitely is something up there. Revert to infrared and see if you see anything.'

Joe: 'There is something there.'

Reid: 'Who is there?'

Joe: '10-12.'

Reid: 'Everyone on alert!'

Joe: 'Copy.'

Reid shouted into the radio calling dispatch.

'This is 287-Sinclair at stakeout location. We have a 10-12 and possible 10-29H on location. We request assistance ASAP.'

Dispatch: 'Roger that. Dispatching assistance.'

Reid: 'Joe, can you get the guys to do a 10-59 around the premises and get back to me.'

Joe: 'Roger that.'

'What's going on out there, Reid?' asked Martin.

'Seems we have an unidentified visitor on the roof. It can only be seen on infrared light. Joe is using a device that allows people or animals to be observed without the observer being detected. He cannot identify a person or animal on the roof. We have to do a change of plans, immediately. Sharon, call your friend Michael now and see if you and Marcus can stay at his house until we all leave for Ireland. This place is no longer safe. Martin, take Christene and go stay at Sharon's house. Make all the arrangements from there. I will have a car take you to where you need to be. You will be safe at Sharon's as long as she isn't there. Karen, we will still follow up on our plans.'

There was another thud on the roof, and a visible crack formed along the ceiling from one end to another. 'Please everyone move quickly,' shouted Reid.

Sharon ran to her room and flung a case on the bed while calling Michael. She could hear sirens in the distance and knew more officers were on their way. Marcus waited by the door for her because he wasn't about to let her out of his sight. Karen called the O'Gradys next door at the flower shop to let them know she will be out of contact. Donna would be coming to work every day, and if Marie or Kenneth could check on her from time to time, she'd really appreciate it. Martin and Christene were standing at the door, waiting for their lift. They wanted to get out of there because it was beginning to look like the ceiling was going to fall through.

Karen looked out the bay window and could see police everywhere. They seemed perplexed for they could not see the perpetrator. Only when given the infrared binoculars, they could see movement on the roof. No one could really make it out, but they could see something. Sharon and Marcus were ready and standing at the door as well. Reid shouted in the radio to shoot at will so as they could keep whatever it was occupied while they all slipped out. Martin and Christene were whisked away in an unmarked police car while Marcus, Sharon, Reid, and Karen went in Reid's car.

Sharon looked back out through the car window, and Karen's place slowly disappeared from the view. She couldn't resist looking on the roof. And she could see it as clear as she had seen it in her room. Standing there pounding on the roof was the same dark creature that tried to strangle her not long ago. It was so angry, and she wondered why it wanted to be so bad.

Marcus put his finger under her chin and turned her head slowly frontwards. He does not want her seeing such evil, for he knew what it was and what it was capable of. Adonai had told him.

Chapter Eleven

Michael Waters

MICHAEL WAS BORN in Ballina, County Mayo, Ireland. Ballina is a big town in the north of County Mayo. It lies at the mouth of the river Moy, Parish of Kilmoremoy with the Ox Mountains to the east, and the Nephin Mountains to the west. The population of Ballina is 10,086, and it is Mayo's second largest town after Castlebar. He attended Scoil Phadraig School, which is a catholic primary school. He hated the school as the teachers practised caning. They would give five or six slaps on the hand. Corporal punishment is a no-no in today's society. He couldn't wait to get away from there.

Everyone in Ireland speaks English, but in a cosmopolitan way. You're likely to hear chatter in a variety of accents from polish to Korean to Japanese to Brazilian. You have to keep your ears open to pick up on it. The Gaelic language in Ireland is a Celtic language, and it is one of the oldest and most historic written languages in the world. Its poetic flow can be heard in schools across the country and throughout the shops, pubs, and streets of the Irish-speaking regions. You have to pay attention because you will see all the street and road signs in the Republic of Ireland in both English and Irish. Northern Ireland doesn't have both languages on their signs.

Michael's early memories in Ireland was only when he was about five or six. His first job was doing the newspaper run. Unlike the United States where the kids ride bikes and throw papers at houses, he had to carry his papers and shout out on the top of his lungs, '*Evening Harold, Evening Press.*' It wasn't a great paying responsibility, but it was something to do and get pennies doing it.

Michael first left Ireland when he was at the tender age of fourteen or fifteen to go to London and work to help out his family. Because of his early departure, he didn't speak the Gaelic. He grew up fast and became a travelling man. He loved to travel all over the world. So far he had been to Vietnam, Australia, Thailand, and many places in the United States as well as Egypt and Mexico.

He liked to dress in a way that gave off the impression he was intelligent. His neck adorned a gold chain and a silver chain. He was oblivious of the fact this clashed, but he did not care. He sported a remote brown moustache albeit the fact he had a full head of white hair. Mike had a gentle old soul, but he was a very confidant and hard working man. He always thought first, though, before acting because he demanded the best possible outcome in any given situation.

It was six years ago when he first met Sharon, during his travels. They both were staying at the Hotel Pennsylvania in New York City. He was there to see a boxing event across the street at Madison Square Garden. She was there on a buying trip with her sister, Karen. They accidentally bumped into each other in the lobby of the hotel. Unlike normal practices most men used to meet a woman, this was truly an accident.

Once he apologised for his blunder and offered of reassurance from her that all was well, they hit it off right away. And when he heard of her Irish connection, he knew he would want to be her friend. It was a friendship that would last a lifetime. From that day to this, he had put himself in her path.

Sometimes, he had to create an opportunity for conversation, dinner, or just a long walk. He was there at her disposal. However, most times, she found him. She was always looking for advice, and he was more than happy to supply her with it.

So when Sharon had called and told him she needed a place to stay for a few days, he was more than happy to allow her to use his house. He was astonished to hear about the events going on in her life. Sharon arrived at the house with her sister and a police officer and another man named

Marcus. After introductions, the three men went into the kitchen to talk. There, Reid explained everything to him and what they knew so far.

'Who would want to harm Sharon and why is her hair so white?' he asked Reid.

'Sharon woke this morning with white hair. We are all surprised by this as well, to say the least. The change hasn't affected her beauty, though.' Marcus confirmed by nodding his head.

'We still are not sure who is behind all this, but we are working on it. There are a few leads thus far, but we don't know who hired these guys. Karen and I are going over to the hospital to talk to one of the suspects. We'd really appreciate your assistance in this matter. Only Marcus and Sharon seem to know what we are dealing with here, and we need Sharon to be safe, in order for us to figure it out. I hear you're from Ireland. We are all travelling there soon and could use your insight about Ireland. Anything you could tell us about Croagh Patrick Mountains would be very helpful.'

'I can do better than that. I am going home in a day or two. I'll meet you somewhere and take you on a tour of the mountains. Why are you so interested in Croagh Mountain?'

'We are not sure. Sharon says she needs to go there. She is having visions or something and is told this is where she needs to be. We all will find out when we get there.'

'Well, the mountains in Mayo, Ireland, are religious mountains indeed. Some believe St Patrick himself was buried on the top of Croagh Patrick Mountain. Croagh Patrick is a holy mountain and stretches over 5,000 years from Stone Age to present day. I can give you more information of this mountain when you visit there. But for now, I can tell you, it has a magnificent view of the surrounding countryside, with one of the highest peaks in the west of Ireland. It rises almost 3,000 feet into the sky above Mayo.'

'Well, we don't need the services of an orographist when we have Michael,' Sharon said, smiling at the door. Karen and she were at the kitchen door listening to the men.

'This is good. It cuts back time wasted looking for one. Good thing you had a friend from Ireland who was also smart, Sharon,' said Marcus.

'Well, Marcus, I believe Michael's friendship was by design. Everything happens for a reason. It applies to us when we met. It was by design. You were at the right place, at the right time when we met.'

'I hate to be the one who breaks this up. We can reconvene later and finish the mountain lesson then. But for now, Reid, we have to go.' Karen turned and took her sister by both arms. 'You be careful. Don't go walking off by yourself again. I mean it, Sharon.'

'Don't worry, Karen. You can trust me. I won't let her walk anywhere,' chided Marcus. 'That's why I am here, to watch her every move.'

'I have to go too,' said Michael. 'She will be safe here. This place has an alarm system that's the best in the world. Modern technology has come a long way. I have spent a fortune on the latest state-of-the-art alarm system as well as a panic room. If something goes wrong, Sharon will be able to lock herself behind a triple-bolted steel door. Once inside, she will have a direct line to the police and be able to monitor the intruders with the help of CCTV cameras. I assure you, Sharon will be safe here.'

'This makes me feel better leaving you here. I am relieved,' said Karen.

Reid and Karen went off on their mission while Michael gave Marcus and Sharon a crash course of the alarm system and a tour of his house. His house was a four-bedroom, two baths split-level with room for adding more bedrooms or expanding. Lord only knew why he had so much space. He was a single man living in this place all by himself.

'I have a home in Mayo an exact replica of this one. I will retire there one day, and I won't have to take anything except my personal things. I try to make life easy.'

'You have a beautiful home, Michael, and yes, it is very secure and comfortable. I like it,' informed Karen.

'Well, I suggest you all stay in my home in Ireland. It's just like this one and not far from the mountains.'

'That's very kind of you, Mr Waters. I am sure Detective Sinclair will be pleased to hear that.' Turning to Sharon, he said, 'Maybe you should call your parents and let them know before they make hotel reservations.'

'Great idea, Marcus. Love it when you're on your toes,' Sharon smiled jokingly at him.

Chapter Twelve

Reid and Karen

KAREN AND REID arrived at the hospital within thirty minutes of dropping off Sharon and Marcus at Michael's. Reid was given an update of events at Karen's store and found out the ceiling had come crashing in. It wasn't long after that, Joe had noticed through his infrared binoculars that the unknown visitor had disappeared. The police was now in the process of clearing the scene.

Obviously, Karen wasn't happy about this news. Her insurance didn't cover unknown visitors. She would have to call the O'Gradys again and bring them up to speed. The store could remain open, but no one would be allowed to go upstairs. It was unsafe for anyone to go up there.

They went up to the ward, which housed the man who had a fence stuck in his groin. Karen could think of a lot of corny jokes to say to someone like that, but she didn't dare while Reid was standing right there.

There was a cop standing outside his door with his head buried in his phone. Reid walked right up to him, and the cop felt uncomfortable at being caught with his head down.

'Relax,' said Reid. 'We are here to speak with the suspect. Put your phone away and come inside with us.'

They all walked inside the room. Karen had to restrain herself from laughter. He was bandaged on his left leg from his knee all the way up to his stomach. His leg was suspended just a little in the air, and he had to lie on his right side a little bit. Karen could only imagine what he must have looked like on that fence. She needed to get that image out of her head. *Get a grip,* she thought to herself.

They walked up to the bed and looked down on him. He opened his eyes and looked directly at Karen. She looked like the lady in the park. *Why was she here?* he wondered. His urge to kill her had now left his mind. He no longer had those desires. He didn't even know why he had wanted her dead in the first place.

'Good day, sir. I am not going to ask how you're feeling. I'll get right to the point. Why did you try to kill my sister?' Karen came right out and asked him, staring directly into his eyes.

'Oh, she is your sister. Well, I honestly don't know,' he shrugged.

'Do you remember the event in question?'

'Yes, I remember everything.'

'Tell me about it, please.'

'I can only tell you, one minute I was at this research clinic volunteering for drug testing. They were paying good money for human guinea pigs. I have some betting debts so I couldn't resist volunteering.'

'How much did they pay you?'

'Ten thousand dollars.'

Karen whistled, 'That's a lot. Then what happened?'

'Then I was in the park looking to kill this girl. I thought it was you when you entered the room at first.'

'Why were you looking to kill her? That's all I want to know.'

'I couldn't tell you that if I wanted to. I was shown her picture by a man named Carlton and told to go kill her. That's it. I would have had her too if I didn't get impaled.'

'Yea, that's got to be a pain in the ass. No pun intended,' said Sharon, laughing inside. 'May I ask you your name?'

He was just about to open his mouth when they heard a pop sound and the window came crashing inwards.

Reid was pulling Karen down beside the bed, and the officer in the room ran towards the window with his gun drawn. Reid was on one side of the window, while the officer was on the other with their guns drawn. He yelled to Karen to crawl outside and get a doctor for the man who had been shot. Instead, Karen crawled over next to the bed and pushed the button that called the nurse. The officer bravely looked out of the window and didn't see a thing. They were four floors up. That shot could have come from anywhere.

'No one out there now, sir. One shot, that's all it took.'

'We never should have had him by a window. Call it in.'

'You got that right,' said Karen, standing up and brushing off her clothes.

'What you mean by that?' asked Reid.

'I am just agreeing with you is all. You've got a man at the door for what? To protect him or to make sure he doesn't escape. If it's to protect him, then yea, he should not have been by the window.'

'Listen, Karen, how were we to know someone would kill him?'

'I'm not here to judge, Marcus. I'm just pointing out or agreeing with you.'

'Why don't I agree with you?' Marcus asked, shaking his head.

'I am sorry if I am coming off wrong. It's just that he talked to me and was about to tell us his name. That's frustrating!'

'You're right. It's frustrating. I didn't even think someone would have killed him. I didn't even see him as a victim, but more as a dangerous criminal.'

'Well, the minute I saw him, I knew he had been drugged or something. He appeared to be just as confused as we are.'

'How can you say he was drugged and confused?'

'I looked in his eyes and saw a gentle soul. Eye contact is a way more telling than words will ever be. That man is no killer. He had to have been drugged or induced somehow to want to kill. We can safely delete the name "killer" off his resume.'

'Karen, you're right. I think maybe I better go over the Bermuda police reports again and check if McGregor had drugs in his system. From what I gather, he was an ordinary man with no history of violence.'

'The other thing that's bothering me is if they have sharp shooters to pick off someone in a hospital, then why not just hire the same person to kill Sharon from a distance. Something is not making sense.'

'Hmm, you're right again. Maybe I better get you a job on the police force. My boss would love you.'

'I'd probably drive him mad! I know I can be infuriating at times, but I like to get to the bottom of things before I make assumptions.'

'See, that's what he likes. Assertive people. I tell him all the time that he doesn't hire stupid people,' Reid smiled at his own self-praise.

Karen had to smile at him too. *He is a bit cocky for his own good,* she thought, but she secretly liked him. She decided to ruffle his feathers a little bit.

'Maybe your boss will rethink that when he learns of your disregard for safety and got a suspect/witness killed today.'

The smile evaporated from his face and was replaced with annoyance. 'Let's just get out of here and go to the clinic,' he announced and turned on his heels and walked over to the police officer.

OK, Karen, you have overstepped the boundaries, she thought. He was mad, and she saw this by judging his reaction. She had to learn when to keep quiet and when not to. Her mouth always got her in trouble, but she could not help it. She always said the first thing that came to her head. The drive over was deathly quiet. You'd need a blowtorch to cut the tension in the air. She decided to just sit back and keep quiet while trying to figure out some things in her head.

Karen and Reid walked into the clinic to find a woman sitting behind the desk. Sharon's description of her had been very accurate. This woman looked up as the couple walked in.

'May I help you?' said the woman, staring at them quizzically.

'Yes, I believe you can. My name is Detective Reid Sinclair. This is Karen Lynch. Her sister was in here yesterday, and you assisted her because a man was following her. We are here today to ask your assistance again.'

'I see. Can you hold on for one minute? I will be right back.' She disappeared into the door behind the reception.

'She is probably asking her boss what she should do,' whispered Karen.

Reid just looked at her and rolled his eyes.

They both went and sat in the waiting room, hoping this woman would return quickly. They were in a hurry to get back to Sharon.

The door opened and outwalked a man in a lab coat with the woman not far behind. Reid and Karen rose and went back to the desk. Reid was about to introduce himself, but the man raised his hand and dismissed the introduction.

'How can we help you, Detective?'

'Miss Lynch here and myself came at the request of Sharon Lynch. She said you'd understand. She needs a vial and says it's kept here. Regrettably, she could not come herself as there have been many attempts on her life. That's why the police are involved. She is under protective custody and cannot leave her location.'

The man sighed, 'In that case, Detective, I'd be honoured to assist Miss Lynch.' He turned to the nurse and told her, 'Help them in whatever it is they need. I will be in my office.' With that, he walked off back behind the door.

The nurse put her hand out and indicated the second door behind the desk. 'Please, enter here.' Karen and Reid walked through the door. They noticed it was an auditorium filled with people. The room was bigger than the reception area, and the walls were all white. There was no other door that they could see. There were no chairs to sit and no furniture, just people.

Everyone in the room was dressed in light colours, making it look exceptionally clean. They were all just standing around talking as if they were waiting their turn. Karen leant over to Reid and whispered, 'Wonder what they are all waiting for? This kind of reminds me of the DMV. Maybe we should pull a number!'

Reid just shrugged and walked to the centre of the room. Karen followed him not know why, not as if there was a chair to sit or anything.

For some reason, Karen felt the need to sneeze. When she did, everyone in the whole place stopped talking or moving and then looked at her. Shortly later, they all scattered and ran in all different directions. They disappeared through openings that seemed to appear in the walls. These doors were not visible when they entered the room. Within ten seconds, the entire room was cleared of all the people except Reid and Karen.

Karen cleared her throat as she looked over at Reid. 'What the hell just happened?' she asked him. He gave her one of his comical looks and said, 'Maybe they think you've got a disease.' He chuckled.

'Not funny, Reid. This is weird, don't you think. Over dramatic if you ask me. It was just a little sneeze for God's sake. Whatever it is, I don't like it. I think we should get the hell out of here!' Karen said.

'But we have to find the vial that Sharon speaks of to complete her destiny. We cannot let her down. You go that way, and I'll go this way.' Reid pointed towards a bare wall.

'And you're pointing at what, may I ask? It's all blank walls in here,' she informed him.

'I can see, Karen. Just go over and feel along the walls. They went through a hidden door somehow. Let me know when you find something.'

'OK, boss.' Karen rolled her eyes and pursed her red lips.

Reid turned towards her, wanting to scold her, but he decided against it. Karen was a strong-willed girl. She might just wallop him one. Better let this one slide. With a deep breath, he just moved on towards finding a way out of there.

'Barring that, maybe we can find a hole or something and dig our way out,' he said.

'Now that's the dumbest thing I have ever heard, Reid! Where did you get your brains?' she asked. 'The corner market store,' she said, answering her own question.

'Karen, why are you being so rude and stubborn? Is it that time of the month for you? I don't know what I did to upset you, but I find your attitude unbearable. Please, let's just get out of here like you said.' He moved along the wall to find that unseen door, rolling his hands along and pressing any edges he might find.

Karen chose not to respond. She just did the same on her side of the room, walking slowly looking and searching for a way out. *Where the hell did all those people go?* she wondered.

'What did you say, Karen?' he asked.

'Oh, didn't realise I was thinking out loud. I was just wondering where they all went. Like which way they went and how they got the doors to open.'

'Well, for one, I noticed an opening right here when they exited. There should be a door right here where I am standing. I saw it when they went out. This is impossible. It has to be a way. I cannot even find a seam or crack in these walls,' he told Karen.

'If you think that is impossible, try slamming a revolving door.'

'Oh, now you want to get humorous, huh?'

'Having some humour doesn't hurt anyone. Especially in times like this when I don't know what the hell is going on. It helps me to think.'

'Maybe we should just relax. I don't think we are locked in here or anything. Let's give it ten minutes tops.'

'OK. I agree.' Karen walked off to the left.

'What are you doing now?'

'I am just going to walk around this whole auditorium for ten minutes, starting from the left and work my way around. I am not one to stand in one place for too long.'

Karen walked around with her hands behind her back, thinking as she did. Within minutes, she went flying down to the floor. Cursing under her breath, she pulled herself back up. Reid was on her in no time at all. 'What happened?'

'I tripped I think. Come stand right here for a minute,' she instructed.

They both stood right where she tripped. Sharon started bouncing up and down before they realise it was a sink in the floor. Reid started bouncing on the floor as well, and the floor gave way. Karen jumped away from the sink and saw a hole on the floor the size of a manhole. They both looked at each other and knelt down on the floor beside the hole, trying to stare into the dark space.

'Darn, Reid, this place could use some refurbishing.'

'Hmm, this is no wear-and-tear hole, Karen. Look at the ridge. It's smooth as a baby's bumpy.'

'Put your hand inside.'

'I am not putting my hand in there! You do it!'

'I am not doing it. You're the big man. You do it.'

Reid rolled his eyes and gave a deep sigh, putting his hand inside. Karen watched as he brought up some dirt. Letting the soil run through his fingers, there was nothing. He repeated this a few times until Karen said, 'Someone once said if you find yourself in a hole, the first thing to do is "stop digging". I know he meant it in a rhetorical sense, but I prefer to think he meant it in a literal sense. It's nothing down there but dirt.'

'That's not exactly true,' said the receptionist standing over them. They were stunned she was there and jumped up off the floor.

Reid stumbling for words said, 'Oh, sorry, miss. We didn't hear you come in. The floor gave way under our weight. The department will fix any damage.'

'No need, Detective. We knew this floor would give way one day. Guess this is the day.'

Karen interrupted, 'Excuse me, you said, "That's not exactly true." What did you mean?'

'I mean there is something down there waiting for you to get it out.'

'And what might that be may I ask?'

'It's what you seek. It's down there, somewhere.'

'So you knew we'd find the hole in the floor. And where did all the people go?'

'We knew you'd find it. The people cannot be in this room when it's found. That's just the way it is.'

'But I sneezed, and they left. Why is that? I don't even have a cold. It's the most weirdest thing.'

The receptionist turned and looked directly into Karen's eyes. *Great*, thought Karen, *a soul studier like myself.*

'There is a reason for everything, and everything has a reason. If you sneezed and they left, then it was meant to happen. I cannot help you any further. You're on your own.'

'Wait, just one more question,' said Reid.

'Yes.'

'We sort of lost our bearings in here. Where is the door to get out?'

'It's over there, of course,' she said, pointing at a blank white wall.

Karen and Reid both looked in that direction and saw nothing. The woman was walking in that direction, so Karen followed her. As she got closer to the wall, she could see the opening. The woman disappeared into the opening, and there it was again, a plain white wall.

Not this time, Karen thought. Digging in her purse, she pulled out her lipstick and marked a big X on the wall. She then placed her purse up against the wall and returned to Reid.

'Common sense is not so common,' he said to her.

'Nope, but I got some. Let's see what we can find in this hole,' she said, rolling up her sleeves.

Karen and Reid spent the next three hours digging up the floor. When they found nothing in one hole, it was easy to create another. Jumping up and down on the floor, it would open miraculously beneath them. It looked like a mole-infested backyard. Finally, Reid's fingers touched something. 'Karen, come quickly,' he called out. Karen rushed to his side and put her hands in the hole, helping him to dig. Finally, after loosening the object, Reid was able to wrap his fingers around it and pull it out.

Holding it up in the air, they could see it was the vial Sharon wanted. It was about fourteen inches in height and looked ancient but in good condition. It had a bowl shape on the bottom and a skinny neck with a pour spout on the top. Karen and Reid both rubbed their hands over the vial.

'It's so beautiful,' said Karen.

'Indeed. Let's get out of here!'

They both stood and looked about the room. They saw Karen's purse leaning up against the white wall and walked in that direction. As they got closer, they could see the red X in lipstick on the wall. Karen picked up her purse off the floor and flung it over her arm. Reid took her hand in his, and they walked into the wall as if they were going to walk through it, but the wall opened, and they went through.

Once they got on the other side of the wall, they realised they were on the sidewalk outside. Karen spun around, but there was nothing there, no wall, no clinic, and no building. She gasped and held her chest.

'I am afraid to ask, Karen,' Reid said without turning around.

'Trust me, Reid, you don't want to know. Let's get the hell out of dodge.'

They were back at Michael's house and sitting on the couch with Marcus and Sharon bringing them up to speed on their day.

'So let me get this right,' said Marcus.

'Karen's ceiling has collapsed. The guy who tried to kill Sharon might not have been a killer after all. He may have even been a witness. But, unfortunately, he is shot and killed, right in front of you while you're talking to him. Then, you were shown rooms with no doors, and then you have to dig for this vial. OK, you had a full day, exciting day. Ask us about our day.'

'How was your day, Marcus?' asked Reid.

'Well, we watched TV. Then we watched TV. Later, we watched more TV!'

Karen and Reid started chuckling at their boredom.

'All jokes aside, I like the security system here. Maybe we should get your parents over here. They would be safe enough even if Sharon's presence puts them in danger. After all, we're here.'

'Good idea, I'll call them right away.' Sharon jumped up off the sofa. 'I'd rather hear them snoring next to me than watching TV.'

'Is this wise, Reid? You see what happened at my place.'

'Your place didn't have a panic room. If something jumped on this roof, it would not be able to penetrate the ceiling here.'

'OK, you're probably right. I am not liking them out there all by themselves. At least here, I won't have to worry. All right then, who will go get them?'

'Well, I am not moving. I have had enough excitement for one day,' said Karen.

'No one has to leave. I'll make arrangements for my best guys to bring them over. They are good at losing people if need be.'

An hour and half later, the doorbell rang. Marcus could see it was the Lynches on the monitor. Giving thumbs up to Reid, he wandered over to the door to let them in.

Christene walked in grumbling, 'Go here. Go there. Make up your mind! We are not getting any younger you know.'

'Great, Mom, happy to see you too,' said Karen sarcastically. 'We didn't realise Michael had a security system here. It's awesome, and you're much safer here.'

The Lynches settled down in the bedroom closest to the library. The safe room was behind the library, making it easier and quicker for them to go there if in a hurry. Martin fell in love with the safe room and was astonished by it. He had never seen anything like it. Every room in the house was visible from inside that one room. There were no blind spots.

Later that night, they were all sitting in the living room chatting when Sharon asked, 'A thought just entered my mind. If a shooter from a distance shot and killed that man in the hospital, why didn't they just do the same to me?'

Karen jumped in, 'I actually have a theory about that. It puzzled me too. Let's just say everything we read about Adonai is true. That he has abilities like no other angel and he won't let anything happen to you because he can sense a killer a mile away. Remember when you said that creature came to you in the night and Adonai saved you. Well, if a hired killer were to shoot at you, Adonai would stop that bullet from ever reaching you. Therefore, they need a non-killer or non-violent person that Adonai wouldn't sense danger to kill you. The only way to do that is a drug-induced normal person who doesn't even know what they are doing. That way, Adonai won't be able to sense danger during the attempts. That's why we are all here, to protect you where he cannot. There is a reason for everything and everything for a reason. I have heard that a lot now in the past few days.'

'Karen, you're a genius! That's got to be it.'

'That's exactly it,' said Marcus.

Everyone turned and looked at him. 'Don't ask how I know. I just do is all. Ever since something picked me up off the ground and talked to me, I sense things. It's as if maybe he is inside me.'

'Maybe he is, Marcus,' said Sharon. 'Maybe he is.'

Chapter Thirteen

A FEW DAYS passed with no incidents at the house. The group just lounged around the place waiting for time. They were leaving for Ireland in two more days. Reid had to make arrangements with his boss to travel out of state. Karen had to make arrangements about getting her roof fixed. The O'Gradys were taking care of all the details. Marcus worked for himself and just had to cancel his appointments for the next few days.

Sharon had no arrangements to make and felt like she was in prison locked away in Michael's house. She'd spend most her time brushing her long white hair.

On the third day, the rain came. It rained all day, and they never left the house. Her parents spent most of their time in their room, and Karen and Reid spent a lot of time in the monitor room. Marcus spent a lot of his time on the couch, so Sharon was bored most of the time. Later that night, Karen and Reid were in the kitchen, while Marcus took a nap on the couch, and Sharon went to the window to look out. The wind and rain seemed to be picking up, and she loved to watch it.

The wind rapped all the windows, making them rattle and shake a little. It was very humid and hot and sticky outside. The rain didn't cool things down at all, but she loved the rain. She loved to see the frogs hopping around. They seemed to come out a lot when it rained. Many frog species need an abundant water supply to reproduce so they are jumping at the chance to breed and feed.

Sharon could just stare out of the window into the raining night forever. She loved the feeling of being dry and secure inside when it was all wet out. Sharon noticed a cat walking nonchalant along a fence. He was not concerned at all about being, drenching wet. She smiled as she scanned the streets outside. Then Sharon noticed the cat was not the only one unconcerned about being wet.

Sharon observed two men standing in the road talking so intently. They were so deep in conversation as they shouted against the wind; they hadn't noticed Sharon watching them.

Their clothes were drenched and soaked to the skin, and their hair was dripping wet. Their faces were too far away to be accurately described, but there was no mistake about the mood they were in. They were angry and shouting at each other.

Sharon called out to everyone to come see this. They came running and looked out the window as well.

The men were so into each other's words; they didn't notice the group's eyes upon them. It appeared there was an argument brewing. Their words were muffled, but the guys could see clearly this conversation wasn't going to be pleasant.

As if just realising they were on a public street, one man turned to look around the area to see if anyone was around. He looked up and down the road, and there was not a soul around. He then looked towards Michael's house, but apparently, he didn't see anyone at the window. He just turned and continued arguing.

They all walked away from the window feeling like intruders. Whatever was going on outside they knew it wasn't any of their business, and besides, they couldn't make out what they were arguing about.

About ten minutes had passed, and Sharon decided to turn out all the lights in the living area and return to the window to see if they left. Pulling the drapes back just a little to peep out, she noticed the argument had turned into a full-fledge shouting match. Although it wasn't proper to stare at them, her eyes were reluctant to leave the window. She just couldn't help it. Reid walked by and saw her looking out the window.

'Pokey,' he called out to her in a joking manner. Then in a second breath, he asked her, 'Are those men still out there fighting?'

'Well, if I am pokey, then so are you if you're asking me about the events outside,' she teased back.

'You shouldn't be at the window. It's too dangerous.'
'I turned out the lights. They cannot see me here.'

'As you were then,' he said and walked off towards the kitchen.

She was mesmerised by the state of them. The one guy who was looking around pulled something out of his pocket. Sharon couldn't make out what it was at first, but there was no mistaking that she saw a knife. Even in the rain, you couldn't mistake the silver of the blade. The man had a grim look on his face as he watched the other guy's reaction to the knife. You could see the other guy was frightened, and the first man's look on his face turned into a malicious frown.

Sharon gasped. 'Oh my God!' she shouted out loud. 'He is going to kill that guy.' Covering her mouth in disbelief, she stared at the scene before her in shock and horror.

Reid and Marcus came running just in time to see the guy quickly thrust the knife into his chest and held it there for a minute. His eyes lit up like saucers, and an undeniable fright came over him. He stared at his victim, pulling out the blade in order to drive it in again. The puddles of rainwater under him now turned into a bright red colour.

He fell to the ground in a heap as the life poured out of him. The man leant over the body and rested his fingers on his neck to feel the jugular pump every last blood out of him. He kicked the limp body and walked off, leaving it there to deteriorate with the larvae.

'Reid, do something,' cried Sharon.

'No, Sharon, he can't,' said Marcus.

'But why, a man was just killed and Reid is a cop?'

Karen interjected, 'Sharon, Marcus is right. Think about it. There is something suspicious about this. Why is there a killing right outside Michael's house when Michael told us this is a safe, crime-free area. I realise a man has died here, but I smell a rat, and my nose never lies.'

'Besides, Sharon, the police are already aware of the killing. They are monitoring the house too. It's a ploy to get someone out of this house,' informed Reid. 'I don't know how they found us, but they did.'

'Marcus, Martin, let's double-check all the windows and doors. You girls move closer to the safe room, just in case. Hang out in the library or check the security system. See what else you could pick up on the cameras.'

'I think I will stay by the window to see what he does next,' said Sharon.

'OK, just yell out if you see something.'

The men went off checking all the doors and windows. Karen and Christene went into the safe room to monitor the cameras. Sharon continued to peer out the window. She saw him walking off down the road but stopped and didn't move for a second. He then turned and looked towards the house. His dark, cold eyes landed on Sharon's window. Sharon jumped back and dove for the hardwood floor. Realisation struck when she remembered the man was no one other than the man who had chased her in the park with Carlton. *Had he seen me watching?* she wondered. Convinced he had seen her, her heart raced and fear gripped its hold over her. Minutes passed by.

She called out to her father, 'Dad, I think that guy might be coming this way.'

'Sharon, get to the safe room right away.'

She tried to get up off the floor, but mobility was impossible. Was this shock? She wanted to raise and look out the window, but the spirit being was more willing than the flesh.

Finally, Sharon rose up off the floor on her knees and crawled to the window. She slightly moved the drapes over and focused back out the window. He was no longer in the street and seemingly disappeared into the night.

'Never mind, Dad, looks like he is gone.'

'Still, get to the library. Something is not right. Reid said the police are outside, but they should have seen this guy by now and picked him up.'

'You're right, Dad. Going now.'

Marcus and Reid re-entered the room and asked Martin what was happening. 'Sharon says the guy is still out there. Shouldn't your guys have picked him up by now? I told her to go to the library because something doesn't seem right.'

'OK, let me check into this. You all go to the safe room. I'll be there shortly, just going to make a few calls on the radio.'

Martin and Marcus went to the library and told the women we all had to go to the safe room. When they all were in, Karen went directly to the monitors and checked them all. Sharon and Marcus sat at the table that was in the room. Christene and Martin went to the state-of-the-art security system. They found the button that closed the safe room door, which was a bookcase on the other side of the door. They were ready to push the button once Reid came into the room.

Reid on the other side was looking about the house shouting into the radio. He wasn't getting any responses. Something was definitely wrong. His radio seemed to be dead. Not even a crackle was coming from it. He checked all the rooms, and they seemed secured. But he heard glass breaking, and the sound of an alarm went off. He rushed to the safe room and shouted to close the door. Christene pushed down the button, and the door slid into place.

Sharon looked over at Marcus, but he seemed to be in a different world. 'Something's wrong with, Marcus,' she told everyone.

They all walked over to him and surrounded the table. Marcus's eyes were wide open, but he could not see them. Then he spoke, making Christene jump a little. He startled her.

'Sharon, you thought you recognised that guy earlier, who is he?'

Sharon wondered only for a second how he knew. 'I think he's the guy from the park. He's the one who was with Carlton, holding a newspaper pretending to read.

'I recognised him when he got closer to the house. Only thing is he looks eviler if that possible.'

'Karen, go back to the monitors. You might be able to see him if you manoeuvre the cameras around the house. Christene, see that switch over on the board, and click it towards the ceiling. This will put the floodlights on all around the house,' he explained.

There was a giant screen high on the wall and about ten smaller monitors surrounding the bigger one and a few more on the desk by the controls. They had a view from every angle. Reid picked up the phone that was connected directly to the police station. After identifying himself, they assured him that they were on their way. He explained there was supposed to be officers already outside the premises staking the place out, but he couldn't pick them on his radio. Dispatch said they would try to pick them but to sit tight as more was on their way.

Marcus seemed to come around and walked over to the monitors. When the area was lit up from the floodlights, they were able to see clearly all around. They kept two of the cameras simultaneously flipping between the desk monitors covering the entrances and windows so they could keep an eye on that as well.

'He is outside still,' said Marcus.

'How do you know?' asked Karen.

'I feel him in my bones.'

'How could you feel that man in your bones?'

'It's not a man as a person. Cannot say for sure, but something is inside him.'

Karen and Sharon looked at each other, and then they both looked at their mother. Christene gave them a reassuring look for she knew they were frightened. So was she, but she refused to let the girls know this or Martin either.

They were still watching the monitors when Martin pointed to something on the screen. By the front door, standing in the road, they could see him clear as day. *What was he doing?* everyone wondered, for this man just stood there looking at the door. Was he contemplating rushing the door to break it down? His eyes looked dark and crazed. They could even see spit dripping from the corners of his mouth. Was he drooling with anticipation? His clothes were falling off him, tattered and torn. He definitely wasn't the same man of fifteen minutes ago when he killed another.

Suddenly, without warning, and with lightning speed, he did rush the door. You could literally see the dusk in his wake. His bodies slammed against the door knocking the hinges off and fly into the air. He had tremendous strength. No one on earth should be that strong. The group in the safe room saw this and was amazed. He was in the house. 'Switch over to the inside camera covering the living room and library!' said Reid. They watched intently as this man looked about the room. Then Karen pointed on the monitor to the flashing lights coming down the road. Help was on its way. The man heard the sirens, but he wasn't prepared to leave just yet. He could smell his prey nearby. He just had to get as close as possible before his antagonistic nemeses intervened.

Reid watched him and was prepared for whatever his next move would be. His gun was in his hand and ready to fire if need be. The intruder walked into the library and moved about the room in flashes of speed. *She is here. I know it,* he thought to himself. Alas, she was not alone. For Adonai was with her. But where, he could not see them, but he knew they were both here.

He moved more quickly about the room, going around the whole room about three times. Then he stopped by the library. *They are behind this bookcase,* he thought. He would break it down, but he heard something behind him. He turned and saw about ten police officers standing in the doorway.

'Hold it right there,' one shouted to him. 'Get on the floor!'

The man moved towards them and as if he wanted to walk right past them. The police kept their trained gun on the subject, ordering him to lie down on the floor, but the man kept walking. One of the officers put his gun in his holster and walked up to the man, attempting to place him under arrest, but he was thrown across the room instead. Another officer then shot his taser at him, clipping him in his side. He dropped to the floor and shook from the electricity coursing through his body, but this only lasted for half a minute.

He got back up off the floor with the taser protruding from his side and continued to walk towards the door. Another officer shot him in the leg, and again, he went down to only get back up and continued to walk out the door. More officers followed him, shouting commands, but he wasn't listening. They reached outside, and the police had had enough. They wanted to bring him to a halt. They shot him again in the arm, and finally, the perpetrator stopped and looked at them.

He, too, had had enough of them. His body started to twist and turn and crumbled. The police could see a purple light surrounding him, and out of the purple light came a black mist. The man's body fell to the ground, and the black mist hovered above it. They could see a man's body forming out of the mist, and giant black wings opened up behind him. The form had no face, but they could see red eyes looking at them. One of the officers literally covered his hands over his face, for he didn't like what he saw. The form floated around for a few seconds, standing there looking at them. Finally, his wings started to flap, and he moved up higher and then flew away into the night sky. All the officers stood there watching with their mouths wide open.

They were not the only ones seeing this. All the eyes in the safe room witnessed this as well from the monitors. Karen looked to see if this was being recorded, and seeing it was, her eyes turned back to the screen.

Reid was the first to move. He pushed the button, and the door slid open. He went outside to the officers identifying himself while raising his ID. One officer walked up to him. 'Did you see that?' he asked with amazement, still staring into the sky.

'What on earth was that?' he asked.

'Whatever it was, it has no right being on earth,' was all Reid could reply. He walked over to the man on the ground. Putting his fingers on his neck, he announced this man was dead. Reid searched his pockets and found nothing on him. *Darn*, he thinks. Maybe he had prints on file and yelled for forensics to process his prints right away.

Joe and his team came running up to Reid. 'Dispatch said you was having problems and couldn't raise us on the radio. We never heard your calls and never saw anything suspicious until dispatch radioed us.'

'It's OK, Joe. This case is simply weirder by the minute. Did you see that thing?'

'Yes, I saw it. What was that, sir?'

'No clue. Maybe the same thing you picked up on with your infrared binoculars the other night. I think from now on, you should wear them at all times. He won't be able to hide from you then.'

'Right, I'll make sure everyone has them on and get you a pair as well. I'll be back in about an hour. I have to check on my men I had up in the trees, sir. They are not responding to me.'

'OK, keep me posted, and if I don't respond, come right away.'

'Will do, sir.' And he walked off into the dark.

Reid walked back to the house, and he could see Karen waiting at the door. He was taking a serious liking to this girl. After this was all over, he might just ask her out on a date, he promised himself.

He walked up and stood beside her, looking out at the scene before them.

'OK, Miss Smarty Pants, what do you make of that one?' he asked her.

'That my dear friend was Aza,' she informed him.

Chapter Fourteen

Azazel

REID LOOKED QUIZZICAL at Karen. 'Aza who?' he asked her.

'Aza is not a who. Aza is short for Azazel. Come indoors, and I will explain more.'

They walked into the house and checked on everyone. Reid called for them all to gather around because Karen had a theory as to what exactly took place. They all seated in the kitchen because Karen liked it better in there.

'OK, first of all, I know you all saw that thing. The police saw it too. I have to give them the videotape later so they can go over it. Otherwise, their bosses won't believe what they say,' Reid started up first. 'Karen just told me this thing's name is Aza.'

'Karen dear, how would you know his name?' asked Christene.

'Mom, a lot of people my age would have heard about him. We did a study on him in my religious knowledge class back in high school. Some view it as folklore, and some consider him a cast-off. I personally prefer to call him the Devil's reject.'

Karen took a deep breath and a sip of her tea before continuing.

'He is also known as satan's ex-right-hand man or a fallen angel or demon. You can see his name in the Bible only three times. It's believed he was cast out into the desert as part of the Day of Atonement. Azazel was the leader of a group of fallen angels called Grigori. These angels liked the look of women on earth and took them as wives, and they bore children with them.'

'I think I read somewhere about that. Weren't they giants though?'

'Maybe, we will all have to look it up and see what we could find. Aza was accused of teaching people to make weapons, thus his being cast out of heaven by God, for God didn't want people killing each other. Satan sort of adopted him into his graces, but soon he disappointed satan as well since he went on to teach men how to make knives, shields, and breastplates made of metal. Satan didn't want to have people praising Aza for the learning of weapons, so let's just say, satan fired him. Aza being fired by satan angered him, but he wanted to get back in satan's graces. Aza and the Grigori degraded the human race by bringing on corruption so as to please satan. He hoped this would get him back in.

'Then God sent his four angels to earth to try to bring back harmony amongst people. Michael, Gabriel, Raphael, and Phanuel saw bloodshed on earth, so they bonded Aza's hands and feet, casted him into the desert, and covered his face so that he will not ever see light, placing jagged rocks and darkness over him. And that is the last he was ever mentioned in the Bible.'

'That means then that somehow, he has been awaken,' said Sharon.

'Yes, indeed,' said Marcus. 'Someone must have found him and brought him back. My guess is, he still wants to get in satan's grace and by doing that is to please him. That's why he is here stalking Sharon. Nothing would please satan more than to stop the Seventh Angel from doing its designed deed.'

Christene looked at Marcus and said, 'You just said "its" designed deed. You said "its". What do you mean by that?'

'I meant "it" as in Sharon, for she will become the Seventh Angel.'

Everyone in the room gasped.

'How do you know these things, Marcus?'

'I am not sure. I just know is all.'

Michael came gushing into the kitchen. 'What has happened?' he asked breathing heavily. 'I came right over when I got the call. Is everyone OK?'

'Yes, Michael, we are all fine. How you got here so quickly?' asked Sharon.

'The security company called my cell the minute the alarm went off. Looks like we need a new front door. I have to call in a few favours if I want this door fixed tonight.'

'Send the bill to the police department. It's our fault because I think the Lynches were followed. We should have been more careful,' said Reid.

'I just want to hear what happened for now. That door was supposed to be impenetrable. It took the experts forever just to install it. You'd need one of the police battering rams to bring down that door.'

'Damn, that guy sure was strong then,' said Martin.

'Honey, that wasn't a guy. Karen says his name is Aza, remember.'

'Guy, thing, Aza, whatever it was. It has a lot of power.'
'Now I got to hear this!' exclaimed Michael.
Michael was filled in on all the events that had taken place. He whistled, 'Why do I always seem to miss the good stuff? So what happens now? What's your next move?'

'I say we should get ready to get our butts into Ireland quickly. What time is our flight, Christene?'

'We have to be at the airport by 7 a.m., so we can leave at 6 a.m. Will you all be safe travelling out in the opening like that?'

'I think so. If what Karen says is true. Aza cannot see light, and we are travelling in the daytime. Besides, I think Adonai is with us now,' said Christene looking over at Marcus. They all followed her gaze to Marcus. Marcus's skin turned beet red. He could not confirm or deny this. He remained silent.

'You all really think Adonai is in Marcus! Hmm, why did he choose Marcus as a vessel, I wonder?' said Reid.

Karen cleared her throat. 'I think Adonai is using Marcus to be closer to Sharon because he knew Marcus has a crush on Sharon, which makes it easier.'

No one spoke in the room. Not even Sharon for her mind was elsewhere.

Reid walked to the door and looked out. The police was still out there. The neighbours in the area had come out looking and wondering what was going on. The rain didn't sway them. *It's people's nature to be pokey,* he thought. Looking at his watch, he walked up to Michael.

'How long before your guys can come over to install a new door?'

'It's going to be a while I am afraid. They have to travel to the factory, pick up the door, and then travel back. With installation, I'd say about two hours tops.'

'OK, then in that case, I think we all better sleep in the safe room for the night. It's the only way to get a full night's sleep.'

'That's fine. I have foldaway beds in the cellar. I'll pull them out. I only have two though. I can take the cushions from the couches and place them on the floor for someone.'

'I'll sleep in the library. I want to keep an eye on the installation of the door. It has to be locked once it's finished.'

Everyone got prepared to get some sleep for the night. Reid actually sat up watching the door being installed. Joe came by to give him the binoculars and inform him two of his guys weren't in the trees where they were supposed to be. They had vanished, and he couldn't find them anywhere, not even on the radio. He had another team trying to track them down. Nothing much else he could do but monitor the house for the remainder of the night.

Karen came out and joined Reid in the library. 'You OK?' he asked.

'Yea, I guess. I just keep thinking about tonight. For some reason, it reminds me about an incident we had with our cat when we were little girls.'

'Tell me about it.'

'You sure? It's a bit morbid.'

'Now I want to hear even more. Go on, tell me.'

'We had a female cat named Arty. Arty slept in the bottom drawer of our dresser filled with clothes for padding. This is where she delivered five kittens.

We were told to make sure the drawer was closed when the female cat wasn't around. One day, walking into the room, I noticed all the kittens' dead. Their necks had been chewed open. Our male cat had killed all five of the kittens. One of us must have left the drawer open. When I looked out the window, the male cat was walking alone licking his lips nonchalant, as if he had done his deed for the day. He had not a care in the world. It took the family months to get over that.'

'Yes, that is morbid. Why would you think of that now though?'

'I don't know. Seeing Sharon looking out the window brought back that memory. Then the look on that guy's face gave me the same chills.'

'That guy wasn't himself. If Adonai is using Marcus as a vessel, then Aza was using that guy. I just wish I had more information about who he was. I told forensics to call me as soon as they knew something.'

'I just hope and pray we are able to get Sharon where she needs to be. I wouldn't be able to live with myself if something happened to her. Or to you even.'

'One thing I am sure of, nothing is going to happen to Sharon as long as Adonai is nearby.'

'If that's the case, why are we here? Why doesn't he just pick her up and fly her to this mountain in Ireland?'

Sharon smiled at Reid. 'If it was that easy, then I am sure he would have done it by now. Adonai is a spirit. Sharon is a human. He cannot pick her up like you could. You see, he cannot protect her from humans. He can only guide us or warn us. However, his powers could frighten away Aza because Aza so fears him. All we have to do is make sure Sharon gets to Croagh Mountains.'

'Then we are special. We are needed. We are wanted by him.'

'What you are is God's gift to you. This gift is for your loyalty. What you make of yourself, that's your gift to God. We will travel wherever we have to if that's where God wants us. God knew you would be at that window that day when you first saw Sharon. Everything happens for a reason.'

'I remember. I am glad we met, Karen. This experience has changed me somehow. I only wish the best for you and your family.'

'All we need is to have faith.'

Karen rose up to go back to her makeshift bed for the night when she noticed the binoculars on the table beside Reid.

'May I have a peep through one of those things?'

'Sure.'

'What am I looking for?'

'Click this switch here and look out there. If you see anything blue or red, let me know.'

'OK. What do the colours represent?'

'Blue is usually something cold-blooded out there. Red means it's warm-blooded.'

'But isn't most things warm-blooded?'

'Well, not everything. You might show up as blue if your body is cold, like in the snow or something. Or if it's an energy, we cannot see.'

'You mean like Aza or Adonai?'

Reid chuckled, 'Yea, like them.'

Karen put the glass up to her eyes and looked out. She scanned the room and then turned the binoculars towards Reid.

'OK, you're a bright red. You hot!' she told him laughing.

Reid turned red literally. She had caught him off guard.

'Um, you better go to bed, Karen.'

'Awwww, you're no fun,' she said and turned on her heels walking into the safe room.

Chapter Fifteen

S HARON WOKE IN the middle of the night. Her body didn't feel right. She had urges to go to the toilet. She climbed off the cushions on the floor and stood looking about the room. The glare from the monitors lit up the room looking like moonlight. Turning she saw Marcus sitting up looking at her. He was the only one awake. Sharon just smiled at him, and he smiled back at her. She walked over to the monitors and looked into each one. There was nothing. All seemed normal outside.

Walking out to the library, she saw Reid slumped on a chair, snoring with his hand dangling on the side holding a gun. *Poor thing. Must be awfully tired,* she thought. *He will make someone a great husband one day.* She walked out of the library and looked out into the living room. There was Michael, on the smaller couch lying on his back with his mouth wide open. Another snorer. No wonder she woken up. How could Karen and her parents sleep with all this noise? Looking over at the front of the room, she could see a new door had been erected. It looked stronger than the first one. A steel plate was covering the bottom half. She wondered, *Why Michael feels the need to have so much security?* He never really told her what he did for work or where he got his money from. She never really asked him. They talked a lot in the past about everything under the sun but never what he did for a living. It didn't matter now, she guessed. As long as they were good friends was good enough for her.

She walked into the bathroom and sat on the toilet. The urge to pee was there again. She felt like she was about to burst. However, nothing came out. Her stomach started to burn inside and cramped up, and she leant over holding it, praying for the pain to go away. The pain subsided after a few minutes, and she sat up properly. Her urine started to trickle, and she was feeling much better. *Phew, what a relief,* she thought. What was that all about? She was just happy that the weird feeling had passed. She walked over to the mirror and looked into it. She noticed her colouring had lightened a bit.

Moving her face closer to the mirror, using her fingers, she opened her eyelids so she could look at her eyeball. It all looked normal to her. She definitely wasn't herself, but whatever was wrong, she was not going to find out by looking at her eyeballs. She shrugged and examined her neck, where she found a strange mark on her right shoulder. Using her hand, she touched all over her neck area. She could feel the mark on her shoulder. Was that another keloid? This was her second one.

She removed her robe and could see other marks over her body. What were these strange markings? It didn't frighten her, but she was curious. She could see the old bruises had healed, even though still visible. Her body was definitely changing. Her thoughts were different too. She was the same person, but she had different thoughts and different feelings. She knew more now. How did she know the things she knows? She was no longer afraid, though. She knew what she had to do and how to do it.

Sharon redressed herself and walked out of the bathroom. She was silent as not to wake the others. Walking back into the library, Reid and Michael had not moved an inch. The snoring continued on though. Back into the safe room, she could see her parents sound asleep in the corner on a mattress dragged down from one of the bedrooms upstairs.

Marcus was still awoke and sitting up. *Why can he not sleep?* she wondered. He looked at her when she entered, but neither said a word. Karen was sound asleep curled up on the rollaway bed. Sharon looked into the monitors again and didn't see anything suspicious. She then went back to bed and fell into a deep sleep.

She woke early and saw no one was in the room except her. She got up off the cushions and went looking for everyone. They were all dressed and in the kitchen eating breakfast. When they saw her enter the room, they all sang good morning at the same time. *Hmmm*, she thinks. *They are in a good mood. This is good.*

'Morning. Everyone is up and about so early.'

'Yes!' chided Karen. 'The rain has stopped, and it's going to be a gorgeous day. We got a plane to catch so you best get ready too.'

'Oh, I could sleep forever the way I feel. Hopefully, you all had a good sleep.'

'I slept great!' said Michael.

'Oh, I know you did, Michael. We all knew you slept great. Even the house knew, for it shook. You and Reid both!'

Reid and Michael didn't find it funny, but everyone else laughed.

'I take it you didn't sleep very well, Sharon?' asked Michael.

'I slept good, but I got up in the middle of the night. Checked on the monitors, used the bathroom, and then went back to bed.'

'Yes, it was a peaceful night. Aza must have been tired and needed some sleep too,' smiled Reid.

'Talking about Aza, we best all get out of here,' said Karen. 'Sharon, go get dressed so you can come back and get breakfast.'

Sharon went out of the kitchen and upstairs to where her things were. She needed to pee again anyway, but nothing would come out. Again, there were pains in her belly, and she could only hold her stomach and wait till it passed. After a few minutes, she was able to pass water. Couple of minutes later, while in the shower, she noticed more changes in her body. She then realised what was happening to her and decided to inform Karen and her mom.

Later, she had Karen and her mom came inside the bedroom, for she wanted to tell them something. While sitting on the bed, she informed them her body had gone through some major changes through the night. She explained how she could not use the bathroom without some pain first, and she probably wouldn't be able to go again ever.

Christene gasped, 'What do you mean, Sharon? Not going to the bathroom, that's ridiculous. Everybody has to go one time or the other.'

'Mom,' said Karen, 'what Sharon is trying to tell us is, she will be genderless soon. Time is of the essence. She is changing, and we have no time to sit around and discuss this. Let's just go and go quickly. If you must, talk to her about it on the plane.' With that, Karen walked out of the room. Secretly, she was not happy about what was happening to her sister, but she also knew what had to be would be. It was nothing anyone could do to change the course of what would become history. She went downstairs in search of Michael.

'Michael, when are you going to Ireland?' Karen asked him.

'I'll be there tonight. My plane leaves later this evening. Why?'

'We need to get Sharon to that mountain as soon as we can.'

'I will change my flight to something earlier. I'll call you when I find out.'

'OK, that's great. Let's go people. We need to get out of here in a hurry. We can use my car. It's the quickest vehicle we have.'

'That's dumb, Karen. My car is quicker. I could use my sirens and get through traffic far faster than you. Lord knows, we don't want your driving skills on the way to the airport. We might not make it there,' claimed Reid.

Karen just rolled her eyes in her head.

'But, Karen, Sharon hasn't had her breakfast yet,' said Martin being the worried father.

'Trust me, Dad, she don't need food any more.'

'Huh,' the men said all at the same time.

'I'll explain on the way. Let's just go.'

Less than an hour later, they were all at the airport, waiting in line to be checked in. Martin and Christene hadn't travelled in a while except when they got to Miami a few days ago. The security system had tightened, and changes had been drastically put into place. The people in the queue were hardly moving forward. They could see the airport security police was heavily armed with vicious-looking dogs. *The world definitely has changed if this type of security is needed to protect people from our own race,* Martin thinks. *How and why have people gotten so mean to each other?*

They were all standing in the queue waiting their turn to go through security. The airport police were walking up and down with their dogs. Suddenly, one of the dogs started snarling and growling, and his handler was having a difficult time to hold him still. One of the other guards walked up to the officer enquiring about what was wrong with the dog. He had no clue and decided to just let go of him, hoping he would take them to the problem. The dog ran off towards the automatic doors. The doors opened, but he didn't leave. He just stood there barking madly outside. People were walking in and out of the automatic doors, but the dog remained put and still looking out. The officers stood behind him, watching and wondering what had riled the dog up so much.

Karen, watching this, said to Reid, 'I think you should pull out your special glasses.' Reid's face lit up like a bulb had been placed over his head. Grabbing his binoculars from his carry-on, he trained them over to the doors. Staring intently into the glasses, he slowly moved them around looking for any sign of energy that he missed without them.

There were loads of red shadowy figures moving about, but that was just the people rushing around. Then on the top of a short pillar just outside the door, he could see it. Taking the glasses away, there was nothing there. But returning them, he could clearly see it. 'Yes, Karen, he is here.'

Reid got out his phone and called the office. He needed a favour, and he knew just who to ask. Within minutes of hanging up, they could hear over the intercom being called.

'Will the Sinclair party please come to the front desk next to check in.' Reid, picking up his case, told them all, 'That's us. Let's go!'

They all walked out of the line, and off to the right there was an airline agent at a closed counter waiting for them. 'Are you the Sinclair party?' she asked. 'Right this way.'

She swiped their passports and moved them quickly down the ramp in front of all the other passengers. They were the first ones on the plane and in first class. No doubt Christene liked the best, for she booked the tickets. This would be the first time for Reid.

Meanwhile, in the airport, the other dogs had started to howl. People were holding their hands up to their ears. It wasn't the loudness of the howl but more so the annoyance of it. 'What is going on with these dogs?' shouted one of the guards. 'Will someone shut them up?'

As soon as he shouted that, all the dogs went quiet. The airport took over an eerie silence. There was a dark cloud surround the airport. The automated doors swung open and in walked a man with a briefcase. He was a bald man with a clean-cut goatee, dressed in a dark suit with an ominous look on his face. He definitely wasn't a happy man. He walked into the airport and walked past all the people in queue and directly up to security, which brought attention to himself.

'Hey,' a lady shouted out, 'I have been here for half an hour now. That man cannot go past me like that. He needs to get to the back of the line!'

Security perked up and agreed with her.

'Sorry, sir, you have to get to the back of the line.'

How dare this mere human tell him to get to the back of a line? Aza thought. But he did as he was told. He didn't want to alert Adonai he was here. Walking to the back of the line, he absorbed all the angry glares he was getting, for he would remember every one of them. He promised himself. It was a good thirty minutes past when his turn finally came up. He walked up to the security and was asked for his passport. The man looked confused. Again, he was asked for his passport. He didn't have one. He was then asked what flight he was intending to fly on. All Aza could do was point to the plane he knew his prey was on.

'Sir, that flight is now full and will be taxing down the runway in five minutes. You will not be getting on that flight.'

Aza saw red. He felt like wringing the necks of each and every one of them.

Then one of them said he would have to catch the next flight out, advising him to get his passport sorted.

Aza hit his pockets and pulled out the wallet with the man's licence in it.

Glaring at the men in front of him, he said, 'Right.' And he walked off back out the doors.

Chapter Sixteen

Croagh Patrick Mountains, Ireland

THEY ARRIVED IN Ireland on schedule. Sharon, her mother, and Marcus slept on the plane. Marcus was really tired, as he had been awoke all night watching Sharon. This was one of the reasons Adonai chose him, for he knew Sharon would be well watched. A limousine was waiting for them to take them to Michael's house. The driver had a sign up saying 'Reasons' written across the placard. This was due to Christene. She didn't want her last name on a card at the airport. Anyone in her group would know immediately it was for them. They all followed Christene to this man, and he took them outside, where he gave them each a cellphone.

'Wow, Christene, you are the best at making arrangements,' said Reid.

'Just wait till you see what's in the limo waiting for us, and then you can pat me on the back,' she smiled at him.

'You're scaring me now,' chuckled Reid.

They all piled into the limo and sat back to enjoy the ride. It was going to take about an hour drive to Michael's house in Mayo. Christene got two bottles of champagne from the fridge. Martin pulled out the glasses.

'Here you go, Reid. A nice glass of bubbly for you to enjoy.'

'Oh no. I cannot possible drink today. I won't pat you on the back after all. This is not a time for alcohol. It's not a holiday,' said Reid.

'Well, I disagree with you, Mr "police officer",' Christene said to him sarcastically. 'This is the first time and probably the last time I will ever travel with my kids, and I may never see one of my daughters again. Besides, I am sure God won't mind a little drink,' she said and then looked over at Marcus.

Marcus looked at her and realised she was looking for his approval. 'Christene is correct. One drink won't hurt anyone.' He reached for a glass.

'All right, all right. One drink! Don't know how I let you talk me into this. But I will join you in a drink.'

They all had their glasses filled, and Martin raised his glass and said, 'To Adonai,' and glasses were clinked together. 'Adonai,' they all said together. Karen's Miami phone suddenly broke the toast by ringing. After a few minutes on the phone, she hung up and said, 'I am shocked I get reception over here. That was Michael. He is rushing to try and catch the next flight over. We are going to have to send the car back to pick him up.'

The door to the limo opened, and it was the driver. He wanted to talk to Reid so he got out of the car, and Karen followed him. She was not letting him out of her sight, for she wanted to know everything that was going on. The driver informed him there was a police officer here wanting to speak with him. His name was Garda Dillon Thorpe. Most police officers in Ireland were referred to as Garda, they learnt. Garda Thorpe informed them that he had been assigned to them during their stay in Ireland. If it was anything they need, he would be their 'go to' guy. But the main reasons were so they abide by Irish laws.

'How do you even know I was here?' Reid asked him.

'Your boss, sir. He called and informed us. That's normal courtesy between police departments in ally countries.'

'See, Reid, your boss is smarter than you think. I'd like to meet him one day,' said Karen.

'Yea, he is smart, all right. He probably just wants to keep an eye on me,' he replied. Looking at Dillon, he enquired, 'Do you travel with us then?'

'That's the idea, sir.'

'OK then. Come. I want to get out of this airport. Don't like being out in the open like this.'

Michael wasn't exaggerating; his house was exactly like the one in Miami. They felt like they never left the States. They checked out the security system here, and yes, it was exactly the same. All the windows, doors, and furniture were an exact replica. They all went about the house, exploring and claiming. Sharon, however, was happy to remain in the safe room and sleep on the floor where she could see the monitors. It was clear and obvious that Aza was not in Ireland. But they were going to act like he was. It was always best to be prepared.

Even though it was still early, she made a bed on the floor by pushing together cushions from the couch. She faced the monitors and lay down on her back watching the screens. She didn't mean to but she fell fast asleep.

Reid and Dillon were in the living room, discussing police stuff. Karen and Christene were in the kitchen, fixing dinner for everyone. Martin and Marcus were in the garden, chatting. The house seemed peaceful.

In the mean time, Michael was on the plane flying over the Atlantic. The plane was only half full. First class had only six people in it, while economy was maybe about fifty. Michael was reading his book when a man walked by him and stopped and sniffed the air. Michael slowly looked up from his book and saw the guy staring at him. *Darn the eyes,* he thought to himself. He better looked away. He turned his head back to his book, but he was not reading. All his senses were on alert, for he knew this was not right. *Why on earth is this man staring at me like this?*

The flight attendant walked by and asked the passenger to get back in his seat. 'Sir, if you're not going to go to the bathroom, please return to your seat. We need to keep the aisle clear.'

The man backed up, continually looking at him. Michael looked up and saw the man was still staring at him. He read his eyes as saying, 'I could kill you.' But Michael didn't have one enemy he knew of. This could only mean one thing. This man somehow sensed he was a friend of Sharon. Wasn't he sniffing the air? Did he have traces of Sharon on him? They did hug when she left. He decided to call Reid right away. Just in case, his suspicions were correct. He made a series of calls, for he didn't want to be followed when he arrived. He told Reid about his weird experience on the plane.

'It's the most weirdest experience in my life. I thought I was going to die just by looking at him. I had to turn my head. Thank God the flight attendant came by and shooed the guy back to economy.'

'Just be careful. If he was sniffing the air, it's probably Aza in that man's body. He has the capability to use people as a vessel to travel around. If he leaves the body, you won't be able to see him. The good thing is, he cannot see in the daytime if he did leave the body. You need to be extremely careful.'

'Don't worry. I know how to lose this guy. Let's just say I have friends. I won't come to the house just in case though. I'll send a car to pick you and Karen up to take you to Croagh Mountain. I will meet you there in a few hours.'

With the new plans sent in place, Michael felt like he could relax more. He had a group of guys meeting him at the airport. They were experts in protecting people and losing any pursuers.

Aza was sitting in his seat when he got a whiff of Sharon. *Don't tell me she is on this plane*, he thought. He sniffed around the air and looked up to first class. Yes, the scent was coming from there. He threw down the magazine and unbuckled his belt. Walking slowly down the aisle, the scent got stronger.

He had to duck his head a little to enter first class. Yes, that smell was coming from here. Walking down further, he stopped at where the scent was strongest. But it was a man sitting there reading a book. This man must know Sharon. His nose never lied to him. That was how he knew they were at the airport in the first place. He smelt her. This only meant one thing. He was going to meet her. He would follow him, for he had long lost Sharon's scent once she left him behind in Miami.

Michael dosed off for the remainder of the flight. It was the flight attendant who was gently shaking him back into reality. They landed at Knock Airport on schedule. Once Michael was off the plane, he called his guys. They were just outside the main door they assured him. Michael walked right out to them, leaving his suitcase behind. He was whisked off but not before his protectors saw the guy whom Michael had warned them about.

Aza was having a hard time to keep up with Michael. *Damn*, he thought. His prey had jumped into a car and was gone. Aza jumped into the first available taxi and ordered the driver to follow the car, pointing to the car Michael was in. The driver was so frightened of his passenger; he shakily did as he was told. The traffic was heavy along this stretch of road, making it difficult for either of them to rush out. Once

Michael's car was able to get on the exit, they sped off. The taxi was maybe about six cars behind, and Aza shouted at the driver, 'Speed it up!'

A third car came out of nowhere and slammed into the taxi spinning it around. This caused other cars to jam brakes, and they all hit each other. This was a intentional accident, Aza felt. He got out of the taxi and looked in the distance for Michael, but he was long gone. Sharon's scent was also gone. But he had no worries; he would roam this place at night, hoping to pick it up again.

Michael arrived at a secure location, and the first thing he did was get a shower. Putting his clothes in a plastic bag, he told his cousin to take them to another town. 'Give it to a thrift shop if you have to.' His cousin gladly took the clothes, but he wasn't going to give away the clothes to any thrift store. He thought to himself, *An expensive suit like that.* He was going to keep it for himself. As if knowing what his cousin was thinking, he said, 'You cannot keep it. The scent on it will bring that guy to you.'

His cousin walked out of the room and opened the bag, placing his nose up to it; he smelt nothing but an old faint scent of aftershave. Yea, he was going to keep it; tucking the bag under his arm, he walked to the car and threw it into the boot.

Michael looked at his watch and realised he had little time to get to the mountain to meet Reid.

A car pulled up outside Michael's house and honked its horn. Reid looked at his watch and called out Karen.

'Karen, the car's here. We have to go!'

Karen came running dressed in her jeans and steel boots she found upstairs.

'What on earth you have on them boots for?'

'Michael said to not wear heels. I have no other shoes here. Besides, I hear that mountain is rugged.'

Reid rolled his eyes and said, 'You could have easily worn a pair of Sharon's sneakers.'

'This is true, but now I have boots, so let's go!' she laughed.

They arrived at the base of the mountain. Karen looked up but could not see the top. It was covered in clouds.

'Michael said to meet him near the visitor's centre. It's called Teach na Miasa at the base of the mountain. Let's go find that,' he told her.

They found Michael leaning against a railing waiting. There were a few people around, but it was busy at all. Michael filled them in on his little adventure. 'I for one would not have been able to sleep knowing that creep was on the same plane with me.' Karen screwing up her face exclaimed.

'I am getting the feeling he doesn't want to mess up the body he is in so he is playing by all the rules. How's Sharon holding up?' Michael asked.

'She is changing. Her body is changing. I'd say we only have one day left before we can get her here. My dad wants to show her where he grew up, so he is taking her to visit his old stomping grounds.'

'Isn't that dangerous?'

Reid chided in, 'She will be all right. One of Ireland's Garda is there and of course Marcus. Hopefully, we get back before they leave. How long does this take?'

'Normally, it takes about two hours for the average person to reach the summit and one and a half to descend, but we won't be going all the way to the top. I just want to show you what to expect when Sharon gets here and to give you some history. It's advisable to wear raingear and sturdy footwear.'

'See,' Karen said to Reid tapping him on the arm.

'Also, climbing sticks are needed. You can buy them at the Teach na Miasa.'

Michael told them all he knew about the mountains. They learnt more from inside the centre. Karen found this walking stick in the centre that looked just like a staff Moses had used on his trip up a mountain. She just had to buy it for Sharon. Standing at the base, Michael said, 'People gather here to celebrate the beginning of harvest season. It was on the summit of the mountain that St Patrick fasted for forty days, and its custom has been passed down from generation to generation. At the top, there is a modern chapel where confessions are heard. Individuals come from all over the world including climbers, historians, archaeologists, and nature lovers just to see the majestic view or study it. Traditionally, locals visit the mountain every year on the last Sunday of July. This is called "Reek Sunday". The other traditional days are the last Friday of July. This is known as Garland Friday. Then there is August fifteenth, which is the Feast of the assumption of "Our Lady into Heaven".'

Karen was absorbing everything she was learning. She loved history no matter what country it was.

'This is a good time of year to see or climb the mountain. Occasional showers blow in over the bay so that's why raingear is advisable. The mountain rises to a height of 760 m above the sea level. Normally, it takes about two hours for the average person to reach the top, but in Sharon's case, I understand she is going further.'

They spent the next two hours at the mountain. Karen wanted to reach the top, but she got this nagging feeling that she should go back. After about an hour of climbing, she told the guys she wanted to go back. 'I get this feeling something is not right. Something is wrong back at the house.'

'OK, let's go back then. Call the house on our way down and check in.'

Sharon called and was informed everything was fine. Sharon and her father had gone to the town where he grew up. The Garda and Marcus were with them.

'Mom, I am coming to get you. Then we are going to go get Sharon and Dad. I have a bad feeling.'

'OK, Karen. Call them and check in if it will make you feel better. I will be ready when you get here.'

Reid called Martin's phone, and he assured them they were fine. They were just walking along the old streets of Milltown.

'Karen is feeling uneasy, Martin. Maybe you should get back into the car and come back.'

'It's such a beautiful day out, Reid. We won't go too far. Marcus and the Garda are here. We are being very careful.'

'OK, but we are still coming to where you are.'

With that, they both hung up.

Chapter Seventeen

Martin Lynch Passed Away

MARTIN WANTED TO show all of Ireland to Sharon, but their time was limited. So, he chose to show her the village in County Galway in which he was born. Milltown is situated on the banks of the river Clare. They decided to walk along the cobblestones sidewalk in the town. He was yakking away filling her in on the history of Ireland, as he knew it. He was giving her so much information, and she absorbed everything he was telling her.

The first thing people think of when they think about Ireland is leprechauns or Irish dancing, but Ireland is so much more. It's filled with rich beautiful landscapes and old castle ruins. Ireland has also given the world some very famous people: Pierce Brosnan, actor; Paul Hewson, better known as Bono from the band U2; Oscar Wilde, a famous Writer; and then there is Maureen O'Hara, a famous actress of her time. Martin wanted Sharon to know everything about the

whole of Ireland for he was very proud. As they walked along
the way, holding hands, he told her many stories about his
country. He was thrilled to bits and excited she was there with
him. He was so intent in their conversation that it wasn't till
the last minute he noticed a car rushing towards them.

To his horror, the driver was ramming right for them. It
was nothing he could do to stop it. Martin had a millimetre
of a second to get his daughter out of the way. He pushed
Sharon to the kerb, and she went flying down on the
cobblestones, but he didn't have enough time to get out of
the way of the speeding car. It struck him with such force that
he went flying up into the air. His body came flinging back
down to earth with such a fast thud that it brought some
of the tarmac up of the ground and into the air. As he was
flying, he knew this was his end. He thought of Christene,
the woman who had chosen him to spend all her life with
no matter how short it was turning out to be. Christene had
chosen him, to bear his children. He felt so blessed to have
been chosen by her. He was now prepared to pay the ultimate
price for the saviour of one of the kids. This was his way to
renovate all his mistakes he made.

Sharon had seen her father got struck by the car and
thrown up into the air and landing on the ground with a
tremendous thud. Sharon screamed and shouted out for
her father. Running up to him, she found him lying on the
ground bleeding from his head. His body was twisted, and

his legs were facing in opposite directions. Sharon knelt down beside him and placed his head on her lap.

Looking down on him with tears streaking down her face, she cried, 'Dad, Dad, Dad!' He turned his head and looked up at her. He saw his daughter as if for the first time. She had a golden colour with the whitest hair flowing around her shoulders. There was a glow about her. His daughter was the most beautiful creature on this earth. She was an angel, and he could see this now. He whispered, 'Sharon, you're so beautiful. I can see your wings.'

Sharon, crying and looking at him, begged, 'Please don't die, Dad. I cannot do this without you. I need your guidance. Please, Dad, please.'

Martin reached his hand out and wiped away the tears from her face. 'Don't cry, Sharon. Be strong. You must carry on without me. There is a reason for everything, and everything has a reason. Always remember that.'

Sharon heard her name being called, and she looked up and saw Adonai standing there looking down on them both. There was so much love in his eyes; it put Sharon more at ease. Martin looked over and saw Adonai. This was the first time he had seen him. Upon seeing that he now had the ability to view Adonai was confirmation for him that he had done the right thing by saving Sharon. Adonai was real, and Sharon needed to continue with her task for a better world.

'Sharon,' he whispered, stroking his daughter's cheek, 'you must continue with your journey. It's imperative you see it to the end. For I have seen him, he is real and his powers are strong. You are his servant, and you must do this deed for him. Please tell your mother thank you for all the years she has given me. I love you all and would love to remain here with you, but I must go now. Give Karen a giant hug for me. Goodbye, Sharon, Adonai is waiting.'

Martin closed his eyes, and she could feel his head relax on her lap. Sharon saw the grave look on her father's face. This would be the last look she would ever see on her father. She imagined her mother's face when she found out the news that her beloved husband had been killed.

Her tears had stopped flowing, for she now knew her father was with him. She watched as Adonai walked up to them both; bending down, he wrapped Martin in his giant wings and lifted him up in the air. The twirling misty lights surrounding them were visible to everyone witnessing this, but it was only Sharon who could see the figures in the centre of the circle of lights. Her father was now in a floating upright position beside Adonai. It was a mystical apparition that evaporated into thin air.

Sharon rose up and walked to the kerb. Looking back, she now could see ambulance attendants pumping on her father's chest. When had they got there for she had not seen them?

A police officer had walked up to her and wanted a statement. But she was in a daze and could not speak. The Garda asked the officers on the scene to get a statement another time. Sharon wasn't in a state to answer any questions.

She could see Christene and Karen running towards her with Michael and Reid behind them. *How did they get here so quick?* she wondered. Karen reached her first, while Christene ran to her husband's side. Sharon could hear her mother's wails ringing through her ears.

How was it that Martin would come all the way to Ireland to pass away in his motherland? This was his country for he loved it so much. He had so much love for his country and wanted to show it off to his wife and kids.

Sharon and Karen sat on the kerb, comforting and hugging each other, while the Garda stood over them. Christene stayed with her husband's body until a special van came to pick it up. There was no need for her to go with it as they were taking it right to the morgue. They all travelled in the car together back to Michael's house. The car ride was quiet and sombre. It was Marcus who broke the silence.

'If it's any consolation, Christene, I am sorry for your loss, but he is in a good place. He said to tell you thank you for your honouring his life by being part of it.'

'Thank you, Marcus. That does help.'

Nothing else was spoken until later when they got to the house. They had to make a decision and make it fast. Karen had a feel of the mountain and related her experience and knowledge to Sharon.

They had decided to get Sharon to the mountains as soon as they could. Her father would have wanted it that way. Their mother's grief in losing him was a very hard thing to witness. His death would not have been in vain. They would all travel there immediately.

Chapter Eighteen

AZA COULD NOT believe his luck. After roaming sniffing the air, he had finally picked up her scent. He had left the body in the bushes because he was able to float around at better as his true being. He would go back later to get his body. He silently moved closer to the scent. He didn't want to get too close for he knew Adonai might be near. Yes, there she was getting into a car with others. She was going somewhere without that cop.

Aza rushed back to his body and re-entered it. He found a car and stole it, driving quickly to where he had seen them. It wasn't hard now to pick up the scent as he knew the general direction of which he had to go. And there she was, walking along a cobblestone street in Milltown. Her arm was locked around the gentleman she was walking with. They were chatting and did not see him in the car slowly following them. He watched them carefully until he saw his opportunity when they stepped off the kerb to go across the street. This was his one chance. He revved up the engine and rushed towards them.

At the last minute, he saw Marcus watching him with Adonai standing beside him. It was too late for Marcus to do anything, but Adonai rose up into the air and came flying towards the car. Aza could feel the car hit something but wasn't sure if he caught his target. The car went on and slammed into a building. It completely crushed the body he was using, making it easy for him to escape it.

He rose up from the body only to see Adonai hovering over him. Adonis's eyes were closed, and Aza knew he was praying to his God for assistance. He was aware satan would come to his aid if he prayed for him. Adonai turned to mist, and the mist swooped down on him, surrounding him, and sucked him up into a ball.

The ball went flying into the air as Aza was once again thrown into the desert of darkness where he belonged to.

Chapter Nineteen

Conversion

THERE WERE OLIVE trees surrounding the base of Nephin Mountain. The olive tree is an evergreen tree. It is estimated that there are 825 million olive trees worldwide. It is the connection to the world's past and its future. When God first visited Adam in the Garden of Eden, he gifted him an olive tree.

God gave instructions on how to care for this tree for its purpose was to produce oils, which would heal man's wounds and cure all ills. The group noticed a path running between the olive trees leading up the steep hill. That path was not there yesterday when Karen and Reid had visited. It was twisting and winding all the way upwards as far as the eye could see. Jagged rocks and bushes were protruding out on each side of the path between the trees. This was no ordinary path. No man would be capable to go up this mountain alone.

They all stood at the foot of the mountain to say their goodbyes to Sharon. All of them were a little scared for her and of the unknown. They were watching in anticipation of what was to occur. They were looking forward to seeing the transformation that they would never see again in their lifetime.

Sharon felt the need to hug each and every one of them. She turned and looked at Reid.

'Thank you so much, Reid, for looking out through your window and seeing me in distress the other day. Without your assistance, I would not have made it here today. Please take serious care of Karen. She is headstrong girl, but more delicate than she thinks. Remind her every day, she is not bulletproof. You have to be strong for her and for your future. For it will be a future filled with danger and intrigue indeed. May God bless you.' She gave Reid a big squeeze.

Turning and looking at Michael, her heart melted with the warmth of his smile. With tears welling up in her eyes, she said, 'Michael, you have been my rock. God alone knows what I would have become if I had not met you. God does know, therefore he has graced us together. You have saved me from what we will never know. Only he would know. Everything has a reason, and there is a reason for everything.

You have always been my voice of reason. You have been my reason for living. Thank you for all your words of wisdom! I will miss our chats.'

Michael looked at her with his smiling blue eyes.

'Sharon, you have been my reason as well. You're the reason why I am the man I am today. I shall refer to you as "Reasons" from this day forth. Rest assure, we will see each other again,' stated Michael. Holding her head in his hands, he said, 'Goodbye, Reasons,' with tears in his eyes.

Sharon looked at him quizzically. *Wonder what he means by 'we will see each other again,'* she thought.

Walking over to Marcus, Sharon took both his hands and swung them in an outward motion and stated in a raspy voice, 'I recognise what your thoughts were, Marcus. I am sorry things didn't turn out the way you desired. Guess, it just wasn't meant to be. Besides, for in the new world, only Nephilims will be allowed. But I am sure your future will include someone who will love you the way you desire to be loved. Simply remember to make the same sum of love back. Goodbye, Marcus, and thanks for everything.'

Marcus was a little embarrassed, to say the least. All he could do was smile in return and hug her back.

Often, parents would worry about leaving their children behind. Saying goodbye to them was a very hard thing to do. But it was the child here finding it hard to say goodbye to the parent. Sharon's mother, Christene, had given her life. Christene had accepted her duty as a mother far beyond any woman's expectation. She nurtured her and protected her all in the name of not just maternal instincts but for mankind as well. She was truly a good woman deserving of everlasting bliss. She would be etched into Sharon's heart in all eternity!

Christene, however, was unsure about Sharon's departure while Sharon was more than ever sure she had to go.

'I have to go, Mom.' Sharon reached out and wiped away the tears from her face. 'Don't cry. I will be OK. We will meet again. I promise you, so don't worry about a thing. God will be watching over us both.'

'I sure wish your father could be here today. He would be so proud of you, Sharon,' said Christene. She was crying uncontrollably now.

'Dad knows Mom. He is here. He sees what's happening, and he wants you to be happy. Don't be sad, for you will join him soon. Be strong. This is meant to be. Everything that's happened in our lives was meant to happen. It was our destiny. It is God's will.' Sharon hugged her mother for what seemed like eternity. She then brushed her hair and stared into her eyes.

Christene saw the love there, and the feeling of calmness washed over her. The tears subsided, and she now smiled at her daughter. No further words were needed between Mother and Daughter, as there was an unseen mutual understanding of each other.

Sharon turned to Karen. Just then Karen remembered the staff she had purchased.

'Hold on one second, Sharon. Got something for you,' Karen told her.

She rushed to the car and picked up the long staff and passed it up to Sharon.

'This will help you on the journey, Sharon,' said Karen.

Sharon reached out to retrieve the staff from her sister. As she took it, their hands touched. There was a small charge of electricity transferred between the two girls. Karen was not frightened. There was a calmness surrounding them both. She seemed to know what Sharon was thinking. She heard her say the words 'thank you' without even speaking it. Sharon was somehow communicating with her. The two of them just stood there looking into each other's eyes. It was obvious to the others, they were communicating somehow.

They were talking to each other without speaking. Their silent goodbyes were something private between them.

Karen chose this opportunity to ask her, 'What will become of us all?'

Karen didn't even realise she asked this question in her mind, and Sharon understood what she was asking.

'There will be angels everywhere guarding pure people and all children. These angels have been assigned by God to minister to all children. You can be certain that they will be protected. Only the evil and murderers and false prophets will be affected by the changes made here today. God is a loving God. He will see no harm come to those who don't deserve it. For those that believed in him shall not perish.'

'What will happen to all the people who have sinned? Will they go to hell?'

'God would never create such a place to inflict on his people. Eternal burning is not and will never be an option. His preference is to just start over. Make a fresh new world. In order for him to do that is to destroy the old world.

'After death is judgement. If they die pure, then they will be raised up with him on the last day. If they die as a sinner, then they will go to hell. Hell is not a place of eternal fire as most people have said for centuries. It's more a place for tormented souls that God has no need for in the new world. Once there, their soul will become nothingness.'

'As for me, I am a Nephilim for now, an angel on earth, but I will soon become a spirit angel. I will exist no more the way you know me to be. I will be neither a woman nor a man, just a genderless spirit being. I had been created only for the purpose to serve for the sake of those who will inherit the earth after the destruction.

'If you come upon an angel on earth, they will be a Nephilim. After destruction, there would be many Nephilims roaming the earth. You will be here to guide them. That is your destiny. Many will come to you. Your wisdom will help them in their mission. May God bless you, my darling sister.'

Karen grabbed her sister's hand. She felt the warmth emanating from her. Karen could swear she noticed something angelic in Sharon's face. There was a glow of light surrounding her. The conversion had begun.

'Goodbye, Sister. I am sure we see each other again soon. I love you,' Karen tearfully told her.

Sharon felt a burning sensation in her groin. Her arms and hands became sweaty. Her hair seemed to be heavier. She looked down at herself, and her body didn't look as if it was the one she was used to. It was changing right before her eyes. She was radiating a dazzling white light in a blazing glory. She turned her body sideways and stared at her shoulder blades. Indeed, there was keloid-looking scars springing up on both sides of her blades. She knew her human body was transforming into her angelic being. Since angels were spirits rather than physical beings, she would no longer need this body.

Conversion involved the replacements and additions of body parts. Converting the physical and mental engineering of the human was something only God could do. Sharon would retain her human identity, but would also have her angelic identity infused into her being. The fact that Adonai had chosen her for this mission was the greatest honour. She was happy and pleased to be part of a changing era.

This was a miraculous historic event, about to occur worldwide. Clutching her bowl tightly, Sharon manoeuvred her way upwards, stopping once to look back at the humans who had helped her. She felt an immense love for them. 'Please God, bless these humans,' she prayed in her mind. Turning back towards the hill, Sharon began her long walk up. Using the staff Karen had given her, she dug it into the earth to help her along the treacherous path.

Sharon felt a presence beside her. She closed her eyes and reopened them slowly. Walking beside her was Adonai. He was not going to let her do this walk alone. He was with her at all times. She walked until there were sores on her feet. Adonai looked down at her feet and saw the sores. He took the staff away from her and threw it on the ground and outstretched his arms.

Sharon looked at him and understood immediately what she had to do. She walked into his arms, and he embraced her. Wrapping the cloak around her arms, the two of them floated upwards towards the top of the mountain. The humans below watched, but they never saw Adonai.

They saw Sharon transform slowly into a light green mist and floated up the hill. The path she had taken was no longer there. It disappeared in front their eyes. The olive trees were no more. The trees also seemed to evaporate. Grass returned to the dirt path. All seemed normal.

The group all looked at each other and sighed in disbelief at what they witnessed. Everyone was crying, and neither knew what they should do next. It was Karen who spoke.

'We don't have much time before events take place. We need to get back home.' Turning to the three men there, she told them, 'I love you guys and will never forget what you have done for this family. May God hold all of you in his grace now and forever? Come, Mom, let us all pray.'

The four of them held hands in a circle and bowed their heads. Their silent prayers floated through the air and upwards to Adonai. This would be the last time in this era that the air would be used as a vessel to carry unspoken words.

To be continued . . .

Look for Nephilim 2: Karen's Legacy

Epilogue

For Sharon is the Seventh Angel

SHARON STOOD UP on the Croagh Patrick Mountain. She was up higher than any man had gone for the mountain grew higher. This was where Adonai had placed her. This was his Irish Mountain. This mountain had a natural elevation on the mountain's surface. The ridge of the mountain looked like an underwater mountain having a valley with a rift running along its spine. This type of ridge was characteristic of what was known as an oceanic spreading centre, which was responsible for the sea floor spreading. A mid-ocean ridge demarcated the boundary between two tectonic plates, and consequently a divergent plate boundary was formed. The mid-ocean ridges of the world were all connected and form a single global ridge system that was part of every ocean, making the mid-ocean ridge system the longest mountain range in the world. The continuous mountain was over 40,000 miles long, several times longer than the Andes, and the total height was about 50,000 miles, a mountain greater than the greatest known to man.

Here she stood, arms outstretched over the land. She was in all her glory. Her hair was flowing behind her head. She was looking angelic in all her right. With her beauty, poise, and grace; with wings outstretched, she stared out into the openness. There was a majestic glow surrounding her. She was beautiful and majestic-looking. The Almighty Female was the Seventh Angel. Having every angelic look there was, she, however, was oblivious of this and her self-importance. Angels, who were continually in the presence of God, would have extraordinary beauty because God's glory was reflected upon all that was around him.

She pulled her hands inwards towards her bosom. She looked down at the vial she held in both her hands and took a deep breath. With a little shake in her hands, she flipped the top of the vial. Her wings started to flap in slow, gentle movements as she walked closer to the ridge. Ever so gently, she stretched her hands out over the plains. Looking into the skies, she said, 'As you wish, my Lord.' She then poured her vial slowly out into the air. She watched with a keen eye as the liquid filled the air and turned into a slight mist. Rivets had rolled out moving sideways and downwards. The mist grew from the tiny drops that had come from the vial. They twirled out and onwards. The spill had a mind of its own, for it knew its destination.

And a great voice came out of the temple of heaven, 'IT IS DONE!'

Soon the atmosphere was filled with wind and storm, and a furious desolating whirlwind was aroused by some invisible power. This was the final catastrophe to overthrow evilness, accompanied with tremendous judgements. The contents of the vial were very cool. It was a hot summer day so the sun heated the earth. The heat from the earth rose up and floated into the air. The action of the warm air rising and the cool contents of the vial drifting downwards played a role in the formation of a severe thunderstorm. This would allow the storm to persist for many hours. Flashes of lightning lit up the sky followed by cracks of thunder. The rumbling grew louder and louder. The thunder became deafening. Very quickly, the northern sky turned black with rage. The speed of the black clouds covered mass amount of areas. The wind increased in intensity. Sharon stood there and watched it all unfold. Her hair blew around her, but the storm did not move her. Lightning came dangerously close to her head, but this did not perturb her.

Sharon knew that the vial had to be poured into the air because it was known that satan used the air and wind as a vessel to send messages to his posse of devils. The territory and powers of the darkness had been dwelling in the air, encompassing the whole earth. The content of the vial cleansed the air and broke apart the branch of the antichrist. The pouring of this vial was the execution of divine wrath and vengeance upon them all. This vial would be the conclusive battle of Armageddon when the remains of all Christ's and his church's enemies would have a total defeat, and this would be the final end. The Seventh Angel's pouring of the vial's purpose would be to utterly destroy those who have destroyed the earth, even all the open enemies of Christ so that nothing would lie in the way of his new world. Now would be the spiritual reign of Christ and be in its full glory, and the antichrist would be no more.

This would bring in the times of the coming of the son of man. Satan and his posse of devils would have been driven from their territories. The heavens passed away with a great noise, and the elements melted with fervent heat.

The beast and false prophets were and are now not. All the anti-Christian powers had been destroyed. All the angels were called, and the new world was prepared for its new beginning.

The utmost effect of the vial had taken place. The end of all wicked things had been done. By the same 'fate' that made the heaven and earth would disappear, and new heavens and earth had succeeded in their space.